LOVING THE MONSTER WITHIN

CASSIDY K O'CONNOR

Dedication

No one is perfect, we've all made mistakes. I believe we are all beautiful disasters and deserve to find someone to love the monster within all of us.

To my family, thank you for all of your support. You never tire of listening to me discuss my stories and you are great sounding boards when I need you.

The blood was rushing in his veins and he could feel his heartbeat in his throat. Something was following him, it was above him, behind him, it was everywhere and he couldn't get away. With the next turn, he skidded to a stop realizing it was a dead end, the creature had trapped him.

"Who are you, what do you want?"

"Are you scared?"

The whisper was so close he spun around, but no one was there. The only light bulb in the area burst to his left, making him spin again. The shadows grew longer, increasing his terror.

"Come out and face me like a man!" The quiver in his voice belied his confidence.

"You're no man, you are a coward."

This time the voice came from the other end of the alley. Spotting some pipes laying against the wall, he slunk toward them and bent to pick one up. Before he could right himself, the pipe was knocked away and a steel grip closed around his throat, pushing him up against the wall.

"Wh...what are you?" His eyes were bulging, trying to take in the sight that must be wrong.

"I want you to feel the same fear your family does. I want you to feel the pain you have inflicted on them ten times over."

With a punch to the gut, he bent over only to be kneed in the face. The beating continued till he was wobbling on his knees, barely conscious.

With giant wings, the creature lifted off the ground slightly, raising his fist one last time as he stared the man down. "You will never harm another person as long as you live or it will be the last thing you do."

The fist to his jaw caused a crunching noise to reverberate down the alley. The creature flew away, leaving the man unconscious in a puddle of his own blood and urine.

One

"Penelope, another case just came in. Maria is asking for your help."

I can't help sighing as I hang my head wearily.

"Thanks, Consuela, I'll be right down."

As I look around my sanctuary, I'm reluctant to leave and face the crisis waiting for me downstairs. A woman can only listen to so many stories of sadness and violence before fearing for her own sanity. I have worked for the St. Anne's Women's Shelter for a little over a year now and while I often cry with the women and children who come in, I never doubt I'm doing exactly what I should be. I just wish there weren't so many people in need to begin with. When it gets to be too much, I escape to the roof for a quick break. No one else comes up, they believe the statues around the roof are demons. In reality, it's a really old building with cool gargoyle statues spaced all around the perimeter. There is a really large one at the center that I'm particularly fond of and often lay across. I named him Frank because he's big and tough looking and reminds me of my dad.

"Well, Frank, I should have known the full moon would bring in more cases. I'll be back later." Climbing off the statue, I stretch and feel an ache in my lower back. "Man, I need to start bringing up a blanket, you aren't very comfortable to lay on."

I shake my head as I head inside. If anyone knew I named the statues and talked to them they would probably have me locked away.

With a tug, I pull the heavy door closed and lock it up. Consuela is waiting a few steps down from me with a twinkle in her eye.

"So how was your date the other night with the school teacher?"

"I thought it went really well up until he didn't answer my calls just like the rest of them. I am starting to think there is some kind of curse on me. How can I possibly have twelve bad first dates?"

"You aren't giving away the goods too soon, are you?"

"If you are asking if I am sleeping with them and they are hitting it and quitting, the answer is no. There wasn't more than a good night kiss and even that was only with a couple of them."

"I'll say an extra prayer for you at church on Sunday and who knows, maybe thirteen will be your lucky number!"

I chuckle at her enthusiasm, I knew dating would be harder when I moved to the city. I didn't think I would be a complete failure at it though. Maybe I'm destined to be alone and give everything I have serving others. Maybe I should consider becoming a nun? Let's face it, I like sex and not just in a casual once in a while kind of way. My libido is really high and my toys just aren't keeping me satisfied. I need to find a man soon or I may combust.

I shake my head to clear my thoughts and prepare myself for our new guests. If I'm not completely in control of my emotions, these intakes can be much more upsetting for me.

"Okay, let's do this."

I follow Consuela out of the stairwell and to the conference room we use to interview new families. Only the slightest hitch in my step belies my shock at seeing the bruises and bandages covering the woman's face. Even though she is in her twenties or thirties, her face shows the tough life she has lived. Her son is cuddled against her side. He looks to be about six or seven years old, but his eyes that peek at me show a child who has already lost the innocence of youth. Thankfully he looks physically okay. I don't think it will ever get easier to see a battered woman or child.

"Penelope, this is Sarah and her son, Alex. We've just finished the paperwork; can you take them to room 304 and get them some food on the way up?"

Kneeling down in front of Alex, I give him my best smile. "Hi, Alex, my name is Penny. Are you hungry?"

Only the slightest nod tells me he heard. Sarah smiles shyly and stands up with Alex glued to her side.

"Follow me and I'll show you around."

We take a short walk down the hall, I stop and show them the artwork hung down both sides. A lot of the kids here are very talented and deserve to show their creations for everyone to see, even if they don't have their own fridges to hang them on. We enter a large room organized into smaller rooms, my apartment could probably fit in here at least four times over. One corner has tables for meals, another corner has a library and computers, the third corner has shelves of games and toys, and the fourth corner has couches and a large T.V. It's after nine p.m. so there are only a few women and children in each area.

"This is the common area where the families can come together to hang out. You can come down anytime and fix yourselves a snack. Everyone chips in around here and takes turns cooking meals and cleaning the common areas."

I slide a glass of milk over to Alex and hand Sara a bottle of water. "Turkey or ham sandwiches?"

Sarah's timid voice cracks as she says they will both have turkey.

"Good choice, that's my favorite, too. Breakfast is at eight thirty, lunch is at twelve and dinner is served at six thirty."

I slide the sandwiches over and sit across from them in silence. Sometimes silence is more comforting than anything else.

"How long can we stay here?"

"You can stay as long as you need and we have counselors you can schedule time with. We also have a couple of lawyers who donate their time to answer legal questions. We will be here for you as long as you need us. When you are ready to go out on your own, we'll help you find jobs, apartments and anything else you need. I promise you are safe here."

We lapse into silence again and let them finish their food, it doesn't take long and they both anxiously jump up to clean their dishes.

"Okay, let's go see your rooms."

The building is old and the elevator tiny; we squeeze in and Alex eagerly pushes the three buttons when I tell him to.

A quick tour of their living room and bedroom then I leave them to rest. I don't know what they've been through tonight, but I know sleep is the best thing for them now. Who knows the last time they felt safe closing their eyes.

My watch beeps quietly, my shift is finally over, one more thing before I can go home...

"I'm telling you, Frank, you should have seen them. They were pale, scared and exhausted," my back cracks as I stretch in my favorite gargoyle's arms. "These night shifts are killer, I can't wait for the sunrise then I can head home and crash for the entire day."

I lay peacefully watching the sky slowly change color, the city waking up. I love sunrises, they give me hope that today is a new day and something magical could happen. The sun crests over the buildings, shining brightly till I have to look away.

"All right, that's it for me. I'll see you tomorrow, big guy."

Two

"So Alex, you have been here two weeks and I still never see you playing with any other kids. Don't you think it's time to make a friend?"

His shoulder barely moves as he shrugs, I see him looking out the window of the conference room at the kids playing with legos.

"Come on, we'll go together."

Jumping up, I hold out my hand and release a breath of relief when his tiny hand grabs mine. Every kid here has been through similar situations so I have no doubt they will welcome him easily.

"Hey guys, this is Alex. We were wondering if we can join you?"

Marissa, a beautiful girl who has been with us for three months, jumps up with legos in hand.

"I'm building a castle, want to help?"

Every kid stops playing and stares at the block she's holding out, no one knowing what he will do. I can't help the tears stinging my eyes when his tiny fingers wrap around the block and he follows her to the table.

An hour later, we've built the largest castle in the city and my back is killing me.

"Okay, guys, I'm done for the day. I'll see you tomorrow."

"Are you going to see the bird man before you go?"

"What do you mean, Alex?"

"You're going up to the roof to hang out with the bird man, right?"

"Oh, the gargoyle statues? Yeah, I like to sit up there."

"They aren't statues, I've seen them flying around."

Um, okay, he's just starting to open up so I don't want to argue. I am a little concerned, he's losing touch with reality to escape his problems.

"I'm jealous, they've never flown for me. I guess you must be something special."

With a smile, he turns and goes back to playing.

I grab my purse out of my locker and head up to the roof. The bird men are right where I left them, it would be pretty cool to see them fly though.

"Frank, I'm upset with you, Alex says you can fly. I'm hurt you showed him and not me, I thought we were friends?"

The stone gargoyle stares ahead like I'm not even there; maybe I'm the one losing touch with reality. I curl against him and wait for the sun to set, nature sure knows how to paint a masterpiece.

"Well, that's it for me, I have a hot date tonight and if I don't get some action, I may just lose my mind. I need to get laid badly! Keep everyone safe while I'm gone."

******

With a knife to his throat, the poor old man whimpers in terror. He's walked these same streets every day for forty years and never had a bit of trouble.

"Give me your wallet and your watch and I'll let you walk out of here."

With shaking hands, the old man passes them over, praying he will take them and leave. He should have known better, with a hard punch to the stomach the old man doubles over in pain.

As the thief pulls his arm back to punch again, he hears a swooshing noise and spins around. The creature flying toward him can't be real, terror like he has never experienced shows in his own eyes. The vice grip around his throat sends him flying against the opposite wall.

"You think it's okay to harm people that are weaker than you? It's your turn to experience their pain."

With a few punches, the thief is unconscious on the ground. The old man still cowers against the opposite wall, watching as the creature takes out the thief's wallet and empties it before turning, tossing his wallet and watch back to him and taking off into the sky.

The old man can't hold back the moan as he pushes himself up and takes off, leaving the alley behind him. He has no desire to be there when the thief wakes up. His brain unwilling to accept what his eyes saw, he chooses to say a prayer for his savior and forget it ever happened.

Three

With one last look in the mirror, I give myself a nod of approval and head out the door for lucky date number thirteen. I have a good feeling about this one. I have shaved everywhere, only newborns are smoother than me.

The restaurant is just down the block from my apartment, Marcus is standing outside holding a bouquet of flowers. We met last week over a cup of spilled coffee when I ran smack into him because I was staring at my phone instead of where I was going. You can tell a lot about a person by how they respond to these kinds of situations and he was really cool about it. I bought him another coffee and thirty minutes later, we agreed to tonight's date.

"Hello again."

"Don't you look good all cleaned up."

"Yeah, turns out coffee stains aren't really a fashion statement."

"I still feel horrible about that, I wish you had let me pay for the dry cleaning."

"Not a chance, plus if you hadn't plowed into me, we wouldn't be here now and that would have been a tragedy."

Oh, he's good, I am so glad I groomed for this.

"Well, should we go inside?"

His warm hand glides to the center of my back as we head inside. Like a gentleman from the old days, he holds the chair out for me and lets me choose the wine, everything is going perfect.

"Excuse me a minute, I need to use the restroom." He smiles apologetically as he stands to leave.

"Sure, no problem."

As soon as he's out of sight, I grab my phone and text Consuela, letting her know date thirteen is very promising.

My bread is almost gone when Marcus comes racing back, panting and disheveled.

"I'm sorry, Penelope, I have to go."

"Wait, what's wrong?"

He stares over my shoulder, shivers and grabs his coat off the chair.

"I'm sorry, I would have liked to get to know you."

He throws a twenty on the table and just like that, he's gone. What the hell just happened? This is a new record, I ran him off before the first course.

"Ma'am, are you ready to order?"

"Um...I need a minute."

The waiter walks away, clearly embarrassed for me. Do I cause a bigger scene by leaving or just pull up a book on my phone and enjoy dinner? As I decide to pull up a book, a deep voice behind me makes me jump.

"It doesn't make sense for the two of us to be eating alone, does it?"

"It would seem I suddenly have an open seat, if you would like to join me?" *Please don't be a douche...please don't be a douche,* I chant in my head as he moves closer to my table.

"How can I resist an offer like that?" He slides into the chair and holds his hand out to me.

"I'm Chris, and you are?"

His warm hand envelops mine and holds on while staring intently at me. I usually like the clean shaven type but his scruffy blonde hair and stubble across his chin looks good on him.

"What should I call you?"

"Oh...um, Penny...Penelope, whichever."

Come on, girl, stop thinking with your lady parts and use your brain.

"So tell me, Chris, what do you do for a living?"

He smirks, showing off the deep dimples in both cheeks.

"I own a private security company."

Well, that explains the bulging muscles.

"That actually sounds like a pretty dangerous job, does your girlfriend worry about you when you're working?"

Smooth, Penelope.

"If only I had someone as lovely as you to care about my safety."

"Pardon me, would the two of you like to order now?"

Chris tilts his head, telling me to go first. He's about to find out I'm not going to eat small just to impress him, I have an appetite and I'm not afraid to show it.

"I'll have the chicken parmesan with spaghetti and a house salad with the creamy Italian dressing."

"That sounds wonderful, I'll have the same."

Once the waiter leaves, he returns all of his attention to me, his devouring gaze lighting my skin on fire as he takes in every inch of me. If one look can make me tingle, what can his touch do?

"Now it's your turn, Penelope, tell me about yourself."

Over the next hour and a half, we consume two bottles of wine, dinner, dessert and in all that time, we never stop talking. The sexual tension in my body continues to build as his hand grazes mine and our legs touch a few times, which I'm convinced he is doing on purpose even though he looks innocent.

I admit I'm disappointed when the waiter brings the check, I'm not ready for the night to be over. Reluctantly, I pull my wallet out and grab my bank card.

"Don't even think about paying, this is my treat to make up for that other idiot."

"You don't have to cover the whole thing, we'll split it."

"How about I'll pay this time and you can get it next time?"

He wants there to be a next time. Deep breath, don't let him see your excitement.

"I'd be okay with that."

"Can I walk you home? I wouldn't be doing my job if I didn't make sure you got there safely."

"That would be great, thanks." *And if you are a good boy, you can see me to my bed, too.*

With my apartment so close by, I decide it will be the slowest walk home ever.

"You know, for a minute there I was dwelling on what a horrible night it was. I'm so glad you happened along when you did. My night definitely improved."

"Maybe it was fate that brought us together."

All too soon, we arrive at my building. I've never invited a guy up before, how do I bring it up without looking like I do it all the time?

"Well, I guess this is good night."

He leans in and kisses me on the cheek.

"Come upstairs with me."

"It wouldn't be very gentlemanly of me to take advantage of you on our first date."

My shoulders stoop and I look away, embarrassed.

His hand glides up my neck to my chin and forces me to look at him.

"I want to see you again."

"I work tomorrow night, but I'm free the next evening. I can cook you dinner here or we can go out?" *Please, Lord, let him choose my apartment.*

"I would love a home cooked meal."

"Then I guess we have a date."

"I'll wait with bated breath till I see you again."

Four

"Look at you, humming while you work. I guess you had a good time last night? Was thirteen your lucky number?"

Unable to hide my cheesy grin, I grab Consuela's arm and squeal like a teenager.

"I don't know if you would classify Chris as number thirteen or fourteen."

"Wait, I thought you were out with Marcus?"

"Funny story...he took off before we had even ordered. I was contemplating what to do when this other guy came over and asked if he could join me. We hit it off and agreed to another date tomorrow night. Can you believe it? I finally have a second date and oh my god, I can't wait."

I was nearly out of breath when I finished spitting all of that out, Consuela was chuckling as she looked at me like I had lost my mind.

"Chris, huh? What's his last name? Where is he from?"

This stops me in my tracks, I don't remember him telling me anything about himself.

"Ummm, well, I didn't catch it." She gives me a concerned older sister look. "I promise to learn more about him on our next date. I guess I just got carried away in the magic of it all."

"Just make sure you are careful and don't fall for him just because he's the first guy to call you back."

I roll my eyes and nod to show her I'm listening.

"Penny, Consuela, you won't believe it, I have to tell you my good news!"

Shawna, one of our repeat guests, looks happier than I've ever seen before. She has three kids and a bastard of a husband who spends his free time hitting them whenever the mood strikes him. She has been in and out of this place a couple of times; he always talks her into coming back.

"My brother called, he said Pete came by his house and handed him an envelope full of money and showed him his car full of boxes. He looked like death warmed over, covered in bruises and wearing a cast on his left arm. He said he was sorry for everything he had done and he was leaving town. My brother went and checked out our house and sure enough, all of his stuff is gone. I don't know what happened, and I don't care, I am so happy we can finally go home and be in peace."

I hug her tightly, then pull her down to reality, "I'm thrilled for you but how do you know he isn't just tricking you again?"

"That's what my brother thought, too, which is why he didn't tell me about it. It's been two weeks and there has been no sign of Pete. Johnny changed the locks and installed a security system for us, too. He says it's safe for us to come home now."

Consuela makes the sign of the cross, then hugs Shawna, "It would seem you have a miracle, we're very happy for you."

After another round of hugs and tears, Consuela and I help the kids start packing while Shawna does paperwork with Maria. I really do hope this is the last time this family has to be here, they deserve happiness.

"I'm going to go take my dinner break up top, I'll be back in a bit."

Consuela waves distractedly, I grab my food out of the fridge and climb up to my sanctuary. With the lights of the city twinkling all around me, I sigh and lay back against Frank.

"I gotta tell you, big guy, I am having one heck of a good day. One of our families is going home and I had a very promising date last night. Maybe things are starting to look up for me."

After a big swig of coke, a belch rips from my mouth. My hand instinctively goes to my mouth and I say excuse me before realizing I'm alone.

"I think there is something to hanging out with statues, you guys can't really judge me by my manners."

After a few more minutes of silent chewing and star gazing, I pack up and head inside. There's definitely a spring in my step. The faster this shift is over, the faster my date will come tomorrow night.

Five

The anticipation of a second date is making me antsy. Part of me is convinced he won't actually show. When the doorbell chimes, my stomach clenches. With one last glance in the mirror by the door, I take a deep breath and open the door.

"Hi, Chris."

"If possible, you are even more beautiful than the last time I saw you."

"Flattery will get you everywhere, come on in."

As he follows behind me, I try to swing my hips and look sexy. My luck, it probably looks like two cats fighting in a bag. Oh well, he's got to like me for who I am, right?

"So Chris, are you from around here?"

"I'm from South Carolina originally. I moved here for work a few years ago. How about you?"

"I grew up an hour outside of the city, I lived with my parents and my two older sisters. After college, I decided to move out and start my own life."

"I could hear the love in your voice when you mentioned your family, tell me about them."

As I tell him all about my childhood, he helps me carry the food to the table and continues asking questions through the entire meal. We talk about college, my job and my dreams for the future. With the last bite of chicken consumed, he sets aside his napkin and lets out a small groan.

"That was incredible, my compliments to the chef."

"Thanks, I rarely cook since it's just me. Do you want to have dessert and coffee in the living room?"

"Sounds good, let me help you."

I hand him the chocolate cake, plates and forks, then pour the coffee and grab milk and sugar.

"Your work sounds interesting, I didn't even know places like that existed. Do you have a lot of families there?" The curiosity in his eyes is refreshing, it's nice to talk to someone about my work who isn't in the trenches with me every day.

"Sadly, we have more people than we should. It's fulfilling work though, I sleep better knowing I am helping these women and children get away from the monsters who are controlling them."

His eyes squint as he studies me. "So you just automatically assume they are all monsters? Maybe the women are making it up."

"Unless the women are beating themselves up, the guy is definitely bad. Everyone that comes in has the injuries to prove it, not that we would ever ask for proof. We have had some single mothers come in for help because they've lost their homes or been evicted. We will help anyone that needs it."

"It sounds like I've met a real life hero." He leans in and kisses me deeply, I'm surprised there isn't any spark. Hopefully that will come with time. "When can I see you again?"

"I'm back on the day shift for a few days. How about Saturday night?"

"I'll be here at seven."

With one last kiss, he leaves.

Six

"Hi, can I get a large coffee with two cream and two sugar?"

"Sure thing, sweetie, just a minute."

Counting out singles from my wallet, I hear a couple of seniors in the corner getting animated.

"I heard he's seven feet tall!"

"I heard he has knives for fingers!"

"I heard there is a bunch of them that go around in a posse."

"Don't mind those old fogies, they are caught up in all this vigilante talk."

I snap my attention back to the waitress, "What vigilante?"

"Someone or something has been going around the neighborhood beating up the criminals. A few people say they've been saved by him/it. I think it's a bunch of crap and they are just bored but then again, something has sure been making it safer around here.”

“Whether it’s true or not, I guess it’s kind of nice thinking we have our own guardian angel, right?”

“Whatever helps bring people in is good with me, that will be three dollars for the coffee.”

I grab my cup and hand over the money.

“Stay safe out there, don’t get comfortable just because you think someone is watching out for you.”

“I will, have a good day.”

The last two blocks to the office go quickly as I think about Chris and our next date. I glance up at Frank and the other gargoyles and give them a salute as I head inside the building.

“Good morning, Jean,”

“Hi, Penny, can you stop by Maria’s office after you put your stuff down?”

“Sure thing.”

After a quick stop in my office, I head toward Maria's and see Consuela coming out of the adjacent conference room.

"Good timing, it's your turn."

"My turn for what?"

"Some detectives are here asking some questions about one of the husbands."

Curiosity piqued, I head into the room. It's rare for us to be interviewed for a case.

"Good morning, I'm Penelope Harbough." I hold my hand out and shake each detective's hand.

"I'm Detective Sampson and this is Detective Murphy. We want to talk to you about Samuel Cross. Have you ever met him?"

"Cross, that must be Jeanne's husband. No, I have never met him. I have seen his mugshot from one of the few times she actually had him arrested."

"Were you aware he had been hanging around this building watching her?"

My whole body tenses with fear for her. "No, she didn't mention it and I haven't noticed anyone lurking."

"He was found last week in the alley across the street unconscious and beaten to a pulp. When he finally came to a couple of days later, he refused to talk about his attacker. Seeing as she has a restraining order against him, we figured someone didn't like him hanging around here. Can you think of anyone that would do something like that to him?"

"I can think of about fifty people who would have loved to watch it happen but no, I can't think of anyone." Then unexpectedly, I laugh till there are tears in my eyes.

"Beating a man nearly to death isn't really funny."

"No, I know, I'm sorry, actually I was thinking about some gossip I heard this morning and the picture in my head was funny."

"There is often a lot of truth in gossip, care to share what you heard?"

"It's nothing really, there were some people in the coffee shop on Third saying there is a vigilante in the area. I was picturing some middle-aged masked crusader in a knock-off Batman suit taking down Mr. Cross."

The detectives don't even crack a smile. "We'll follow up with the coffee shop. If you see anyone hanging around, please give us a call. What you guys do here is good work, we don't want people getting scared and not coming for help."

"We'll be in touch if we have any more questions."

I shake their hands and head to my office. Before I can even turn my computer on, Consuela comes in and sits across from me.

"You know I don't believe in violence, but a small part of me was really glad to hear about that creep getting his due."

"I'm not exactly broken up about it either. We don't know the whole story though. What if we traded one bad guy for another?"

"Good point, maybe we should talk to Maria about getting a security guard, at least for the night shift."

"Actually, that's a good idea and Chris is in private security, maybe he can recommend someone."

"That's right, you had a date last night, didn't you?"

My shrug answers for me. She gasps and demands information.

"We had a good time, we talked for hours, had a great meal, then he kissed me goodnight and went home."

"You don't seem very enthused."

"I guess I'm kind of disappointed there isn't a huge attraction to him. At first he seemed really promising but the more time I spend with him, the more I notice there isn't a lot of chemistry. I'm going to give it some more time and see how it goes."

"So tell me all about him."

Her question stops me, my mouth opens and closes a few times and I realize we never talked about him. How is that even possible? My job is listening to people, how did I manage to talk about myself all night? Rather than admit I don't know anything about him, I make an excuse about making rounds and escape into the common room.

Sitting by the window, I see Alex crying.

"Hey, little man, what's going on?"

"I heard my mom on the phone crying. I could hear my dad yelling at her saying she couldn't keep me from him," his lip quivered as he lunged into my arms. "I don't want to see him, he hurts Mommy."

"I promise you don't have to see him if you don't want to."

"Maybe the bird man will protect Mommy and me."

He hadn't mentioned them again so I was hoping he had gotten over the imaginary creatures. I rub his back and hold tight till his tears are replaced by quiet snores. There is comfort in holding a sleeping child, their innocence is a soothing balm to our hectic lives. A tap on my shoulder has me turning to face a swollen-eyed Sarah.

"Thank you for watching him, I hope we didn't keep you from work."

"I'm here to help any way I can, I'm glad I could be here for him while you focused on your phone call."

"Yeah, I don't know what I'm going to do. He can afford a lot better attorney than I can, I'm scared he'll win."

My heart breaks for her. I grab her hands that she's wringing anxiously and squeeze.

"We are going to do everything we can to help you."

With a shy smile and a nod, she picks Alex up and heads back to their room. As terrible as it sounds, it's easier when the abuser just gives up and decides not to fight. They have a long road ahead of them.

With a heavy sigh, I pull myself up and start making rounds. There are a lot of other people who need help, too.

****

"Do you hear that?"

"I don't hear anything, just hurry up and put the bags in the car."

With a groan, he lifts the overstuffed duffel bag into the trunk. A fluttering noise in the shadows behind them makes them both turn suddenly.

"I'm telling you, man, there's someone out there."

Both men pull guns out of their waistbands and walk hesitantly toward the darkness.

"Unless you want to get shot, I suggest you step out here now."

"I don't think you want me to do that." The growl sends chills down their backs.

"Wh...what are you afraid of?" The quivering in his voice makes his fear obvious.

A deep rumbling chuckle reverberates all around them, "I don't fear you, boy," The creature steps into the light, a foot taller than them both, cracks its neck and with one shake, giant wings stretch out behind him. His glowing red eyes shine bright in the darkness and ensure they will have nightmares for years to come.

The leader cocks back the gun, raising it higher. The creature responds immediately and with one hard swing, knocks both men into the concrete wall. Their unconscious bodies slide to the ground.

"Fools. Men these days are such weaklings."

He cleans out their wallets of all cash then drags them back into the store they were stealing from. Once they are tied up, he returns all of the store items and pulls the fire alarm to alert the police.

With the wad of cash stuffed in his pocket, he takes off into the sky.

Seven

It's been a week and I've been on three more dates with Chris. I like that he is totally cool with my job and even asks lots of questions. Some men get turned off after they hear what I do, they are afraid that I think all men are bad which couldn't be further from the truth. He never seems worried about it and is genuinely interested.

"Earth to Penny, the detectives are back and would like to speak with you again."

Clearing my thoughts of Chris, I rush over to the conference room.

"Hello, detectives." I shake both hands before sitting across from them.

"We want to thank you for the tip about the vigilante. We asked around and heard the stories, on a hunch we started looking at some of the other cases you have here and come to find out, eight of the men whose families are here have been attacked in the last year. One of them, a Pete Masters, spoke to us over the phone and confirmed he left town after getting beat up as well. The funny thing is, none of them will describe their attacker. They get spooked and shut up real quick."

"I remember Shawna being excited when Pete left town. She didn't seem to know about the attack."

"It would seem the *vigilante*," the detective sneers and uses air quotes, "is focused around this place. We also believe he's responsible for stopping some other crimes in the area as well. He must fancy himself a bit of a Robin Hood. He's been stealing from the criminals and giving back what they've stolen."

I bite my lip to hide the grin trying to spread across my face. I don't really see why the police are bothering with this investigation, it seems like the guy is doing what they can't and that's exactly why they are irritated.

"You're taking this very lightheartedly, have anything to share?"

Their accusatory looks grate me wrong the way. "You don't think I have anything to do with this, do you? I can promise you I don't spend my spare time beating up dirt bags."

"The only thing we can get out of people is that it's a guy so you aren't on our suspect list, we just need to know if you've heard anyone around here asking questions or maybe one of the employees has a husband or boyfriend that is trying to be a little too helpful?"

"The only male employee we have here is Joe Swanson, he's seventy-five and can barely push the mop bucket around. I also don't really hang out with anyone outside of work so I couldn't tell you anything about their husbands."

"Till we know what is going on, you guys should keep an eye out for anyone suspicious and call us if you hear anymore."

I take their cards and head back to my office. A little while later, Consuela hurries in looking excited.

"Do you think it's true? Do you think we have our very own guardian angel?"

"It's a nice thought, isn't it? A large part of me is completely okay with what he is doing. These guys deserve a taste of their own medicine, right?"

"I wonder if we know him. Maybe it's Ben the mailman, he looks really buff."

I chuckle at the excitement in her eyes. "While I do agree with you on his body, I'm not sure that's enough to convince me he's Robin Hood."

"Just in case, I'm going to start being extra nice to him. In fact, I think he's coming today, I have some candy in my office he might like."

She waves bye as she jumps up excitedly. Poor Ben has no idea what he's walking into.

Eight

"Did I tell you about the cops coming to my work a couple of days ago?"

Chris mutes the T.V. and turns toward me.

"They were asking if I knew anything about the vigilante in the area, have you heard of him?"

I study his face, trying to see if he gives anything away.

"I think I did hear some people talking about it a few days ago."

"The cops think he is focused around my work, maybe he's someone connected to one of us."

"That seems scary, do you think you guys are safe there?"

The genuine look of concern on his face gives me comfort that he is not the guy the police are looking for.

"Actually, I was thinking of suggesting Maria hire a guard, at least at night. I'm sure we can't afford your company, but maybe you know someone who would be a good fit?"

"How about you take me through the building, I can give some suggestions on ways to make it safer and once I have a lay of the land, I can ask around."

"That would be great. When would be good for you?"

"I'm good with tomorrow if you are."

"Sure, I'll meet you at the coffee house on Third Avenue and we'll walk over together."

He excitedly kisses me on the cheek before jumping up.

"Where are you going? We haven't finished the movie."

"I want to make sure I'm prepared for tomorrow so I want to head home and do some research."

"Oh well, okay, I'll see you in the morning."

He sure does take his work seriously, doesn't he? I lock the door behind him and go back to the movie, no point in both of us missing the ending.

Nine

"Good morning, Penelope. I ordered already so go ahead and get yours, then we'll get started."

His eagerness is surprising, I guess it's good to have a security guard who likes his job.

Coffees in hand, we walk the short distance to the office and I usher him into Maria's office.

"Maria, this is the guy I was telling you about. Chris has offered to check things out around here and maybe find a couple of night guards for us."

"Glad to meet you Chris. I admit, all this vigilante talk has me on edge. I don't want anyone feeling like they can't come here if they need help."

"Understood, I'm happy to help any way I can."

"Okay, let's get started."

I hang back and let Maria do most of the talking. Once we're through the offices, we head out to the common room.

"As you can see, this area is the heart of the whole place. The kids get a lot of comfort from hanging out together."

Out of the corner of my eye, I see Alex dive under the table and curl into a ball. Running over, I crawl under and touch his back.

"Alex, what's wrong?" As soon as I touch him, he backs away.

"Hank, what are you doing here? How did you get in?"

Sarah's terrified voice comes from across the hall and the panic intensifies with each word. Confused, I look around and realize she's staring at Chris.

"Did you really think you could keep me from him? He's my son and I'm taking him with me."

Nausea hits me instantly, I have a feeling I've been played. "Chris, what is she talking about?"

"Oh, sorry, Penny, guess I lied. Now bring my son over here and I'll leave peacefully."

Anger floods my entire being, how dare he come in here and try to take Alex.

"You're out of your mind if you think I'm letting you take him anywhere."

Rage floods his features, turning his face an ugly red color. Now I understand why I never connected with him, I think part of me knew something was off.

"I'm so tired of you bitches thinking you are so high and mighty, bring me my son!" Spit flies out of his mouth as he takes off stomping toward us.

I drag Alex out and hold him behind me as I back away. Sarah runs toward Chris and screams for us to run. My hands are instantly empty as Alex pulls away and takes off running. Without looking back, I take off after him and my stomach drops when I see him heading for the stairs to the roof.

"Alex, stop, don't go up there. We'll be trapped."

"Come on, Penny, the bird man will save us."

Maybe now is not the time to argue with him on fantasy versus reality; if I want to keep him safe, we need to keep going. I saw Maria run for her office, I'm sure she called the cops already. All we need to do is stay a step ahead of Chris, no, Hank as long as we can.

We burst through the door and shield our eyes from the morning sun. I grab his hand and pull him between two of the statues furthest from the door.

"Just stay quiet and we'll be fine, the cops are on their way."

After a few deep agonizing breaths, guilt washes over me for letting him in and leaving everyone down there to fight him. Alex whimpers as the door swings open and Hank steps out.

"Come on, Penelope, bring him to me and this will all be over. No one else needs to get hurt."

No one *else*? Oh my god, what did he do? I hear gravel crunch and see he's almost to our hiding place. We have no choice, we have to try to move. As soon as we take a step, the gravel crunches and he sees us.

"You can't keep him from me."

"You're a monster, you don't deserve him."

He quickens his pace and we back away till I feel a hard surface behind me. Hank's entire face transforms into a look of horror. Spinning around, a scream tears from my throat. I grab Alex and try to run.

"Penelope, stop, I'm trying to help you. Stay behind me."

"You...you're Frank...but how?"

I watch in fascinated horror as my buck-naked gargoyle statue walks toward Hank, who is backing away just as fast. He grabs him by the throat and dangles him over the building. Giant black wings spread out from his shoulder blades as he effortlessly holds on to Hank, who is squirming and trying to scream for help.

"You are the one who has been eluding me. This ends today, you will leave this place and never speak to your family again. If I see you again, I will kill you."

He tosses Hank against the door and I'm relieved when he slumps over. I don't know what to make of this new threat, dragging Alex behind me as we back away from Frank.

"Penny, stop, this is the bird man. He is helping us."

Alex slips from my grasp and runs over to the naked giant smiling at us. My gaze lowers to his groin and I can't help but gulp, it seems every part of his body is large. He notices my gaze and runs over to his pedestal, digging around and pulling out some threadbare pants and a shirt. When he turns back, I'm surprised to see his face has smoothed out and he looks more human than gargoyle.

"How is this possible? How are you here?"

"It's a long story that I have waited a very long time to tell you. You should get Alex downstairs and come up with a story of how you knocked out that piece of garbage."

"How are you here right now? All this time I've been talking to you, telling you things. Oh my god, the things I told you." A blush spreads across my face.

He takes a few steps toward us when he is thrown to the side by Hank. His face instantly transforms back to the terrifying gargoyle mask. Hank lunges again and Frank spins away, and unfortunately Hank couldn't stop himself and goes over the side of the building.

All three of us run to the edge and look over. With a deep breath, I am relieved to see Hank passed out, hanging from the claw of one of the other gargoyle statues. Part of me wishes he hadn't been caught, the world could do without him in it.

"Penelope, I hear the cops coming up the stairs. You need to say you wrestled with him and he fell over. You can't mention me."

Before I can argue, he is stripping down and climbing back on his pedestal.

"When you can, come back and I will explain everything."

The door bursts open just as he hardens back into a statue. Alex runs into Sarah's arms as the cops with guns drawn ask where he is.

I point over the edge and don't bother turning around as they look over and start laughing.

Sarah makes eye contact with me and I look away. I brought that man in here to our sanctuary. The bruise already forming on her cheek where Hank must have hit her causes another wave of guilt to come over me.

"Ladies, I need to take you downstairs, some detectives would like to talk with you."

With Alex between us, we make our way down to the conference room. Sampson and Murphy are grimly sitting with their notepads open in front of them.

"Ms. Harbough, you can wait outside while we take Sarah and Alex's statements."

With the weight of the world on my shoulders, I slide down the wall and close my eyes. I can't look at anyone right now. I think back to all the time I spent with Hank. It all makes sense now, he pretended interest in my work to gain information and never talked about himself. I am relieved we never slept together, I don't think I could take that guilt, too.

Finally, the door opens and I avoid looking at Sarah as I enter the room.

"Have a seat and take us through how you met Hank and what led you to bring him here."

It only takes ten minutes, I tell them everything that had happened up till now.

"Honestly, he said he was in personal security and everyone was spooked about the vigilante. I thought I was helping."

Sampson hands me a tissue, I didn't realize I had been crying.

"You are a lot smaller than him, how did you manage to knock him over the edge?"

"I didn't, he came at me and I spun out of the way. His momentum carried him over. If he weren't in such a blind rage, I don't think we'd have gotten as lucky as we did."

The lie slips easily from my mouth as I flashback to the man on the roof who is the real hero of the story.

"Well, between the assault on Sarah and attempted kidnapping, we have enough to put him away for a while. Don't be so hard on yourself, your heart was in the right place."

After a few more questions, they let me go and Consuella is in the hall waiting for me.

"Are you all right?"

"Embarrassed, guilty and pissed off, but physically I'm fine. I guess I should go talk to Maria."

"She's in with Sarah and Alex and her door is closed. The roof is clear now, why don't you take a break and I'll tell her you will be down soon."

The roof is my hiding place, my place to go when I'm stressed. Ironically, I'm scared to go up there. Did I imagine Frank came alive or is he really waiting up there to talk to me?

Consuella hugs me and heads into her office. Keeping my eyes down, I quickly make my way through the common area to the back stairs. My hands are shaking as I push open the door to the roof.

Frank is on his pedestal, hard as stone. Slowly circling around to his face, I stare at his lifeless eyes, maybe I'm losing my mind.

I can't help the laugh that bubbles up, how could I have possibly thought he was real?

"What is so humorous?"

Before my eyes, his skin softens, hard lines disappear and the beautiful human face from earlier emerges. Like before, he is naked as he grabs his ragged clothing and sits on the pedestal. I realize he is patiently waiting for me to get control of my thoughts and my breathing. I'm pretty sure my heart is about to beat out of my chest. "I don't even know where to begin, there are so many questions."

"I'll start," he stands and bows to me, "my name is Asald and I've been here for more than a century, but I am much older than that. Somehow you have freed me from this life of stone. It started the first day you came here, I was suddenly able to move, just a finger or toe. Within a couple of weeks, I was able to fully shift into a human. I didn't know what to do with myself at first, then you started visiting so I stayed. I am drawn to you and I think you can feel it, too."

"So you've been living up here all this time? How have you been eating...wait, do you even need to eat?"

"Yes, the hunger came once I was able to fully shift. At first I would steal anything I could, then I started getting some money and was able to buy food."

"How did you *get* money?" I couldn't help putting air quotes around the word get. He's already admitted to stealing, not that I can be too upset, he did it to survive.

"I took it from bad people."

"Wait, are you the vigilante?" The gasp sounded loud in the silence around us, "The one that has been beating people up and stopping crimes?"

His huge grin answers my question. "Are you happy?"

Confusion is written on my face, "Why would that make me happy?"

"The crimes I stopped were simply because I wanted to help someone in trouble and I needed the money. The others were for you though, you told me how much you hate the guys and wished they suffered as much as their families did. Sometimes it would take weeks, but eventually I would find them and take care of them for you."

"Oh geez, I may have said those things, but I didn't actually mean for someone to act on it."

The look of utter bewilderment on his face is adorable. "I don't understand, this is how we used to do it in my time."

"Your time? What are you from, the Medieval times? Wait, don't answer that, I need to take care of a few things then I want to sit down and talk through all of this. I'll come back to get you and we can go to my apartment."

"There is no need to get me, I can meet you at your home."

"You know where I live? Of course you do, why should I even bother asking that? If you can track husbands who have never been here, it's safe to assume you can find my apartment easily."

"It seems like you are upset with me."

I take a deep breath, how do I make him understand his ways are archaic and a little creepy without sounding ungrateful?

"I promise I'm not upset, we'll talk more later. I'll be home as soon as I can."

With one last look of utter shock that this is really happening, I shake my head and go back inside. I can't put off talking to Maria any longer and I really need to talk more with Asald.

Maria's door is open and knocking quietly, I get her attention.

"Can we talk?"

"Yes, I think we need to."

"I am so sorry this happened, I should have never brought him here. I will have my office packed up by the end of the day."

"Penny, slow down, no one is asking for your resignation."

"How can anyone still want me here? In one fell swoop, I made all of their nightmares come true."

"What happened was unfortunate and showed some holes we have in our security. Every person here knows what it is like to make mistakes, to need second chances. Are they scared? Yes, but after a few improvements everyone will feel better. Why don't you take the rest of the day off and start fresh on Monday."

I grab my stuff out of my office and wave bye to Consuela without stopping to chat. I am way too eager to get home and interrogate Asald.

Ten

Looking down the alley next to my building, I am surprised that he is nowhere to be found. Maybe he hasn't come yet, I give in and head upstairs. I'm relieved he's not standing at my door like a lost puppy. As my door is swinging open, I have the brief thought that he somehow got into my apartment. Everything looks the same as when I left this morning. Kicking off my shoes, I head into the kitchen and pour a glass of wine. I might need a few after what happened today.

After a big gulp, I shuffle toward the bedroom and flip on the light. A face is staring in my window. The scream rips from my throat and wine sloshes down my arm.

"Penny, it's me, Asald. Let me in."

"Hold on."

I put my wine on the dresser and grab a towel to clean off my arm. The window squeaks open as I struggle with the rusty hinges. I can't help but shake my head at seeing him lounging on the fire escape with a cheesy grin on his face.

"Jesus, Asald, you scared the crap out of me. Please tell me this is the first time you have been out here."

He climbs through the window and looks slyly out of the corner of his eyes. "Um, yeah, the first time."

My confidence in his answer is lacking. I clean up the wine spilled on the floor and wave him to follow me to the kitchen.

"Would you like coffee, wine, or a coke?"

"I haven't had wine in ages, that sounds wonderful."

I pour him a glass and join him at the kitchen table. For a minute we just stare at each other, my brain still trying to process that this is Frank standing in front of me.

"I'm so confused, I don't even know what questions to ask."

"There is so much to say, I feel like I should start at the beginning. I was born March 13th, 1668 in France. My family were poor farmers and I had very little chance of bettering myself. Every Saturday I would bring food to sell in the nearby towns. There was a beautiful girl who caught my eye. Her name was Arabelle and she came from a noble family, her father was a baron. We were sixteen and in love, but of course we came from different classes so we couldn't be seen together."

My eyes tear up as I see the anguish in his eyes.

"The secrecy was maddening, she swore her father would never allow a match to someone with no money." The muscle in his jaw tenses, his eyes turning angry. "On my way to the village one day, I was approached by a man in a black cloak. He told me he knew of my relationship with Arabelle and he could help us. He said that if I agreed to give him my soul when I died that he could give me money and a title so I could offer for her. The wealth was mine for the remainder of my life. At first I thought he was crazy or some kind of witch. He was very convincing and kept reminding me of all the ways I could be with my love if I just agreed. After all, what is the price of a soul after I'm dead for a lifetime with her? Finally, I gave in and we shook on it."

My wine is left forgotten on the table, his tale so outlandish I'm enthralled and need to hear more.

"He snapped his fingers and a large bag appeared at my feet, I should have run right then, I wasn't thinking clearly. Inside was clothing finer than I had ever touched, money and papers documenting who I was. He told me the money would never run out and we could live happily for the rest of our days. He bowed and disappeared before my very eyes. Not wasting a moment, I ran behind a tree, changed clothes and immediately went to Arabelle's home. Sitting in the salon waiting for her father was nerve wracking. Just because I looked noble on the outside did not mean I felt it inside. She came in with her father and looked shocked and scared to see me. I told him I was a nobleman recently moved to the area and I wanted to court his daughter. After quite a lengthy discussion, he agreed to the courtship as long as I set up house and proved I was here to stay. I think he was relieved that I told him I required no dowry."

He stopped and took a long sip of his wine. My mind was racing, I have read historical romance novels before, I knew most of these terms, how bizarre to be standing in front of someone who lived it.

"After that everything went quickly, I did everything he asked and within a year we were married." His eyes turned sad and his speech lost its excitement. "One year later, King Louis XIV declared war against the Grand Alliance. All lower class men were forced into service and my brother was only fifteen. I couldn't let him go so I chose to go in his place. If it weren't for my new nobility, it would have been me anyway." I could see the anguish on his face, part of me was afraid to hear what came next. "I was gone for five long years and was set to go home within the month but a surprise attack on our camp ended that. I was killed in battle."

I had finally taken a sip of my wine when his last words came out. I choked and red wine sprinkled across the table. He grabbed the towel off the counter and started cleaning like he hadn't just said he died.

"I'm sorry, you were killed? Not that all of this doesn't sound bat shit crazy, but I can't wait to hear how you are standing here in front of me. And where did the gargoyle come from if you were born a man?"

"I remember lying on the field and I knew instantly I was dead. I couldn't understand why I was still aware until the stranger in the cloak showed up in front of me. Soldiers were running everywhere, oblivious to this man hovering over me. He gave me a sad smile and said it was time to collect on our deal. I begged him to give me more time, that I hadn't lived a lifetime yet. He touched my forehead and I was suddenly in a dimly lit cave in line with many other men and women."

My stomach growling loudly made me focus again. I looked outside to see it was completely dark and getting late.

"I'm going to order pizza so you don't have to stop your story. Please, continue."

I open my laptop and order while he picks up where he had stopped when my stomach so rudely interrupted us.

"I stood in that line for many hours, people around me were crying or looking around, clearly as confused as I was. Finally, I was led into a room where a man larger than I had ever seen was sitting at a table staring into a ledger. The cloaked man appeared next to me and told my story to the stranger who stared intently into my eyes. When we reached the point of my death, the cloaked man disappeared and the stranger stood up and walked circles around me.

"*What a shame to sell your soul for love only to be given two years with her. How unfortunate for you.*"

"*Please, sir, if you could tell me where I am and what is going on, I am very confused.*"

"*You seem like a smart man, I think you know what is happening.*"

"*I'm in Hell and you are the devil?*"

He smiled big, revealing razor sharp teeth. "*Very close. I am one of his princes, my name is Lanthos. There is no need for Satan to bother with something as trivial as this.*"

"*Taking my soul is trivial? I beg to disagree, this is a very serious matter. How long will I be here? What am I supposed to do?*" *He circled me slowly, inspecting every inch of me. When his face was inches from mine, it took everything I had not to close my eyes. I was terrified and he knew it.*

"Actually, I have another proposal for you. Something about you is intriguing me, you might be just what I'm looking for to stop the boredom I feel of late. How about this for a deal, you can be released into oblivion where you will wander for eternity, being called upon to be tortured when it is my desire, OR you can join my ranks and be one of my soldiers."

"The first idea sounds positively terrifying, so that's obviously not a good choice. What would I do as your soldier? I've killed plenty in the last few years, spilled more blood than I ever care to again."

The laughter rumbled deep in his chest, "You are in Hell, boy, of course there will be blood. I tire of this job, I am ready to take a break. You will run this process, listen to each person's story and decide what part of Hell they will be sent to. When I am bored and require someone to tease, you will send them to me. Sounds like a pretty cushy job if you ask me."

As I contemplate my choice, I hear screams reverberate through the cavern. That person was clearly only given the first choice.

"I'll do it, I'll be your soldier."

"For the next two hundred years I did as he asked, I acted as judge and jury while thousands of people were brought before me. Some were easy as they did terrible things when they were alive. There were others like me who did nothing except make a deal with the devil soldiers. They were harder, I tried to send them to the best places, well, as best as they can be in Hell."

The doorbell rings causing me to jump. I hadn't realized I was leaning in, heart racing.

"That's the pizza, I will be right back."

The smell is tantalizing and I hurry back to the kitchen, eager to dig in.

"I hope you're hungry, I got a large margherita."

He stared quizzically into the box. Right, they didn't have pizza in the seventeenth century. I grab a slice and hold it up.

"It's dough with cheese, tomatoes, garlic and basil. Watch…"

I take a bite and chew with a smile on my face. He shrugs and pulls a slice out and copies me.

"This is actually quite good, I like this pizza."

Thank goodness I ordered a large, he devours six slices quickly.

"Thank you for the meal, Penny, that was delicious."

"Should we take our wine and continue on the couch?"

"Are you sure you want to keep going? I know it is almost your bedtime and I don't want to keep you."

"First of all, Maria told me to take off till Monday, second, you have to finish your story and third, how do you know when I go to bed?"

"Lucky guess? Now, where was I?"

I fold my legs under me on the loveseat and he sits across from me in the recliner.

"Right, back to Hell, so I spent many years working for my master. I didn't mind most of it, the only bad times were when he asked for someone to be sent to him. I never knew what he did with them but I could hear the screams and they never came back out of his chambers. I tried to relieve my guilt by sending him the worst scum down there, I tried to think of it as getting justice for their victims." His hands fidgeted in his lap, he looked at me nervously, "I don't want to tell you what happened next but it's integral to how I came to be here."

Reaching forward, I cover his hand with mine, a tiny electrical sting making me jerk back. It wasn't unpleasant, just surprising.

"It's the connection, I felt it every time you sat against me on the roof."

"What does it mean?"

"I have a theory, let me finish my story and see if you agree."

I nod and sit back, nervously biting my nail since his warning has me afraid of what happens next.

"Everything went smoothly for a while, I should have known it was too easy. I was summoned to my master's chamber where he informed me he was yet again bored and had a new job to add to my list. He wanted me to learn the art of torture so he could sit back and watch. I was immediately horrified, I begged him to choose someone else. He laughed as he chained me to the wall. I only lasted one day of him torturing me before I gave in, I had to stop the pain."

I could see the emotion in his eyes, the regret, the pain. Tears ran down my face just imagining what he went through.

"I agreed to his job, but begged that he never make me hurt a woman, I could never do that. To my utter shock and relief, he agreed to my terms. He taught me so many unimaginable things and I did things I am ashamed of. He would lie on his bed and watch me torture man after man. When he tired of it, he would heal them and send them to a different area of Hell. He would then call in one of the many women who slept with him and he would kick me out. I liked this part because it usually meant I could have a few days off. I never feared for the women either, they always seemed willing and I only ever heard moans and shouts of ecstasy from his room."

He let out a deep breath and gulped down the rest of the wine in his glass. I didn't say a word as he refilled the glass and drank again.

"This new setup lasted for another hundred years till one day his desires changed again. He wanted to watch me have sex with women, the problem was I hadn't touched another woman since Arabelle and swore I never would. For days he kept me tied to a chair in his room as he paraded one woman after another in front of me and he would laugh when my body betrayed me and I became erect.

"After a week of this torture, he brought a woman in with long, curly brown hair, laid her on the bed and made love to her, then as he came he yelled out Arabelle's name. I was out of my mind from exhaustion, the shock of my wife being in that bed with him was too much. I broke free from the ropes keeping me bound and charged the bed. I grabbed one of the knives I use for torture and buried it deep in his back. He rolled off her and I picked her up only to find it wasn't her, he had tricked me. I should have known the knife couldn't kill him. His roar reverberated through the chamber as he stood at the end of the bed with the weapon in hand.

"Did you think you could defeat me, boy? You are no match for a prince. I tire of you and your undying love for your wife."

He snapped his fingers and we appeared on the rooftop of your work. Everything was so different, I hadn't seen the world in hundreds of years. With another snap of his fingers I was paralyzed, I could feel my body changing and hardening, it started in my toes and worked its way up. I looked down and found claws where my hands were, and the wings that popped out of my back caused excruciating pain. He laughed till all I could move were my eyes.

"Maybe an eternity up here watching life pass by will change you. Your wife remarried, you know, she had five children. Just think, while you were pining for her in Hell, she was fucking another man. Her descendants live in this city. I hope they walk by you every day torturing you with this knowledge. Let's see love save you now."

"He disappeared and I finished the transformation into the gargoyle statue. I stayed like that for over a hundred years, fascinated as the city and people changed before my eyes. I was doomed to live that way till you showed up and freed me."

Eyes wide, I shake my head in confusion. "How did I free you? I didn't do anything."

"I think you are my soul mate, he said love would save me. I felt you the moment you stepped into that building a year ago. No one else came up to the roof except you, you were always drawn to me."

The idea that I am his great love and fate sent me to free him was hard to believe, no, it was freaking impossible to believe.

"I know it is a lot to take in, I've had a year to think this through. Why don't you sleep on it and I can come back tomorrow to talk some more?"

"You can't leave? I mean, you don't have to turn back into a statue every day or anything, right? Are you really free?"

"I have been testing that for a while now and it would appear that I no longer have to be a statue. My shifting ability has not weakened so I assume that is a part of me now."

"Well, the wings are pretty cool so if you had to be stuck with something, that's what I would pick. Why do you think he chose a gargoyle as your prison?"

"He made me into a monster while I was in Hell. I guess he wanted to make the outside as ugly as the inside."

"He was wrong, there can't be anything ugly inside you. Think of all the people you have saved over the last year. If that is a monster, then I would be proud to love the monster within you."

"I've waited a long time to hear those words from you but I know you have heard a lot tonight and I want you to take your time and process everything. If you don't mind, I will take the last of the pizza with me? It's easier than trying to find food tomorrow."

I jump off the couch and pace back and forth, trying to decide what to do. My mind and my heart are saying two very different things.

"Look, this is all crazy and I'm seriously wondering if I imagined all this and you aren't really here. On the other hand, Alex saw you, too, and I do feel the pull toward you as well. It doesn't make sense for you to keep living like a homeless man. Why don't you stay here till we figure things out? And by here, I mean on the couch."

He launches himself at me and swings me into a hug. I guess he likes the idea.

"I would be grateful to stay with you, I am finding it harder and harder to live up there and it turns out when I'm not a statue, I can really feel the cold. I've almost taken enough money to buy a coat I saw in the shop down the street."

"That brings up a good point. While you are here, you can't do any more Robin Hood stuff. I can get you some clothes and there is plenty of food here. No more stealing, okay?"

"If that is your wish."

"Okay, how about I show you the shower and then we can get some sleep. This has been one heck of a day and I am wiped out."

I grab a towel out of the closet and put it in the bathroom. Lucky for him I like big, roomy sweatpants, I give him my largest pair and show him how to turn on the shower and adjust it. Apparently in Hell you don't have to do these things so his face when I show him the running water is priceless.

I leave him to it while I clean up from dinner and make a bed for him on the couch. He's not going to fit perfectly, but it has to be better than the floor or his pedestal. I lay back in the recliner and wait for him to come out. Considering how long it has been, I guess he likes showers.

My eyes open groggily when I realize he has picked me up and is carrying me to my bed. Curious to see what he will do, I pretend to still be asleep. Like a gentleman, he tucks me in, kisses my forehead and goes out to the way too small couch.

Staring at the ceiling, I can't help contemplating the man in my living room and what I'm going to do with him.

Eleven

My eyes pop open to sunlight streaming in through the window. For a minute I lie there listening for any sounds outside my room. I hear the T.V. quietly playing from the living room. Still in my clothes from yesterday, I decide I need a shower, but first I need to check on my ancient guest. I pull the door open quietly, sure I didn't make a noise, but still his head swings around.

"Hi." I give a shy wave and head toward the kitchen. I make two cups of coffee in the Kuerig and head out to the couch.

"I wasn't sure how you drink coffee so I left it black."

"It smells wonderful." He grabs the steaming mug and takes a sip, gives me a thumbs up and continues drinking.

"I was thinking after breakfast, I could run down the street and grab you some clothes. Once you look like you belong in this century, I'll take you out around town."

He reaches down to his tattered clothes on the ground and pulls out a wad of bills.

"Will this be enough?"

I grab the crinkled bills and straighten them into a pile. He has thirty six dollars to his name.

"It will be more than enough. Come on, let's make some grub."

"I'm not sure I like grub, but it sounds interesting."

I give him a tour of the kitchen and show him how to use everything. His innocent fascination with modern conveniences is adorable.

"I'm going to shower, then go pick up some clothes for you. Will you be okay while I'm gone?"

"Yes, I will continue watching your talking box."

"We call that a T.V. and actually, that's a good idea. You can catch up on a lot of how the world has changed."

He refills his coffee cup and hurries out the living room, I guess he's adjusting well.

After a quick shower, I tell him I'll be back soon. His distracted wave goodbye is evidence he is enthralled by whatever crappy day time show he found.

I didn't have brothers growing up and I've never lived with a man besides my father. It feels strange to go shopping for one, I don't even know what kind of underwear he likes. The image of him standing naked in front of me flashes before my eyes and I feel my cheeks heat up from the memory. I really hope I am his long lost love because I desperately want to fuck him. I grab a pack of boxer briefs, a pair of jeans, a couple of shirts, a totally random guess on sneakers and a jacket. Proud of my haul, I check out and head home.

I'm not surprised to find Asald hasn't moved a muscle. I drop the bags next to him on the couch and look at what he's watching.

"Judge Judy, huh? I was thinking History Channel would be better but hey, whatever floats your boat."

"This woman is tough, I like that she doesn't have to torture the people."

"Yeah, these days we're not really into that. It's not good for ratings, you know."

He looks at me quizzically before shrugging and turning to the bags expectantly.

"I got you some very basic things, we'll get more later. How about I throw those rags out and you can take a shower and get changed?"

"I very much like the shower, I'm happy to take another one."

My jaw drops as he stands and strips down, hands me his dirty clothes and marches off to the bathroom. He really isn't shy about his body. Not that I mind, it is beautiful to look at.

Trying not to think about the man in my shower, I busy myself cleaning up the breakfast dishes and straightening his bed. I lay out the clothes for him and wait. He sure does like long showers, my water bill is definitely going to rise.

Finally, he comes out and to my utter enjoyment he is still naked. As he's stalking toward me, I don't notice my breathing has quickened. His hand slides gently down my cheek to my chin and lifts my face to his.

"Thank you for everything you have done. I have spent many months wishing I could be with you but now that I am, I'm afraid it's all a cruel prank and I'll find out I'm still stuck on that pedestal watching life pass me by."

His lips touch mine and the electricity between us intensifies the nerves running through my body. His tongue finds mine and we deepen the kiss. It has been too long since I've been kissed and never as good as this. He pulls back, breaking the spell, and I realize I've wrapped my arms around his back and his erection is pushing against my lower abdomen.

"Tell me you can feel the connection between us."

"Yeah, I definitely feel something..." I'm not sure if he is referring to his dick I'm dying to get my hands on or the mystical love pulling us together. Reluctantly I pull away, all of this is still so surreal and technically I did just get out of a relationship. Even if it was fake and I was being lied to the whole time.

"How about you get dressed and I'll take you on that site seeing tour now."

He nods and dresses quickly. I'm relieved everything fits, although the shoes are a little snug. Like a true tourist, I take him to all the best spots in the city. He marvels at the churches, begs me to stop at every street vendor food cart and I practically had to wrestle him from going on people's boats at the pier.

It really is a perfect day with a perfect gentleman. He is constantly finding ways to touch me, hold my hand, caress my cheek. He keeps handing me things just so he can stroke my fingers.

After a late dinner at a Chinese restaurant, we walk quietly home. Nerves have started to settle in and I'm struggling to stay happy. As we near the entrance to my building, I slow down, trying to drag out the evening.

"I can feel something is wrong, what is bothering you?"

"I'm sorry, I'm trying to be a good tour guide. It's just that I'm going back to work tomorrow and I'm worried what everyone will say."

"Didn't you say Maria is supporting you?" I nod my head miserably. "You have done so much good in the last year, people know that. Give them a chance and you will see that they are not mad. How about I help you relieve some of that tension?"

Instantly my body reacts to his words and I hope he's not just talking about a massage.

He grabs my hand and pulls me down the alley, then halfway down he pushes me up against the wall of an alcove. His large body is blocking anyone from seeing me, not that anyone comes down here anyways. A large part of me is freaking out at the idea of doing something, anything sexual out here in the open, but the louder part of me is insisting this is going to be good so I better hold on for the ride.

With a devilish smirk, one hand glides up to my hair and pulls my head back, exposing my neck and pushing my breasts out. He plants one of his thighs between mine and I can feel his heat through the thin material of my underwear. My clit throbbing almost painfully, I can't help riding his thigh as his mouth moves to my cleavage, stopping just above my nipples.

"Please, I need more," I moan out in frustration.

He chuckles before pulling one large breast up and out of my bra. He latches on as his hand moves up my thigh and pulls my underwear aside. Two fingers glide in my soaking wet folds as his thumb finds my clit.

"I love how wet you are," he growls into my ear. "You are so fucking sexy."

His strokes are slow at first, then quickly speed up. Gripping his shoulders, I let everything go. Every failed date in the last year, Hank's betrayal, all of it melts away when I scream out in orgasm.

My head resting against the wall, I pant, trying to get my body back under control. I love that he holds me, kissing my face patiently while I regain the use of my limbs.

"That was beautiful. You were beautiful."

As my breathing calms down I become aware of what we just did and in such a public place. I have never done anything like it before.

"Come on, let's go upstairs. Hopefully that has relaxed you enough to get some sleep."

He grabs my hand and our fingers entwine as we walk back out of the alley. Maybe something good is coming out of the Hank situation after all.

Twelve

"Penny, you're here. Come on, I need to catch you up."

Consuella is waiting for me at the receptionist desk the next morning. I follow her to my office and stuff my purse in my desk.

"How has it been? Did Sarah and Alex leave?"

Her look of confusion surprises me, I was sure they wouldn't want to stay here after what happened.

"Of course they didn't leave, no one has. In fact, we are being inundated with families from much further away than normal." It was my turn to look confused. "After the story broke of what happened, it also came out about the other men getting attacked and that the cops believe the vigilante is somehow tied to the shelter. Don't you see, these women aren't getting justice through the courts so they think by coming here, the vigilante will take care of their problems. We've also had an influx in donations, we even hired night security."

My head falls onto my folded arms. How can this be happening? Asald was the vigilante, he can't keep doing that though. It's not right and he could get hurt or worse, caught. How do you bail a man out of jail who doesn't exist?

"I'm sure you are relieved, you can relax now that you know everything is okay."

She has no idea how not okay all of this is. These families are hoping for a miracle that Asald simply has to stop performing.

"We have a busy day ahead, go see Maria and I'll see you later."

With coffee in hand, I drag my feet to Maria's office. Even if she is supporting me, it doesn't mean she isn't mad.

"Knock, knock."

Maria spins around and points to the phone, then waves me in. My leg bounces up and down nervously as I wait for her to finish her call. She wraps up quickly and tosses the phone onto her desk with an exhausted sigh.

"That's the fourth reporter I've talked to today. The vigilante story is getting us a lot of attention. Sadly, we need donations so I'm not going to turn away free publicity. How have you been?"

"I'm good, I've been so worried about everyone here. Are Sarah and Alex okay?"

"Sarah is pretty shaken but she feels better with the increased security, and having Hank behind bars helps, too. Alex is fine. He swears the birdman saved you guys, he thinks he is his protector. I guess as far as reactions go, his could have been a lot worse."

Oh god, Alex has been telling people about Asald. I have no idea how I'm going to handle that.

"I'm not sure if Consuella told you but we have quite a few new families to process. I divided them up."

I grab the stack from her and stand up to leave. "Thank you again for being so understanding. I swear this will never happen again."

She smiles and then rolls her eyes when her cell phone rings again.

I take my new workload back to my office, thoroughly review each file and make notes where I can. Really, I'm just stalling, Sarah is out there and I have to gather the courage to face her.

When I have nothing left to do, I grab the pile of files and drag my feet all the way to the common area. Just my luck, Sarah and Alex are watching T.V. and spot me right away.

"Penny, you're back! Have you seen the bird man? He's been gone since the fight, do you think he's watching over Daddy in jail?"

Alex's tiny hand squeezes mine. This poor kid has been through so much in his short life.

"You know what, I bet he is keeping an eye on your dad. He wants you to feel safe here and so do I. I'm sorry I let him in here."

I glance at Sarah, who smiles reassuringly to me. That's a good sign, right?

"Alex, sweetie, why don't you go play with the other kids while I catch up with Penny."

Uh oh, sending the buffer away. Before she can speak, I jump in hurriedly.

"I know you are mad, you have every right to hate me. I'm going to make this up to you guys, to everyone here."

Her warm hand grabs my shoulder and squeezes.

"Penny, please stop, you are talking to the woman who fell for Hank's tricks first. I know how good of a manipulator he is, why do you think it took me so long to leave? You protected my son when it counted and I will always be grateful to you for it. Let's consider the matter behind us, okay?"

Her strong arms wrap me in a hug that releases all the emotions I had been holding back. I'm embarrassed to admit I'm crying, yep, like a baby right in the middle of the common area. I hadn't realized how affected by all this I was. It makes sense though, I saw them beaten and bruised, I knew what he was capable of. I recognize these are the tears of relief.

Once my emotions are back under control, I feel hope and determination flood my body. With my enthusiasm restored, I head off to meet our new families.

Thirteen

With a spring in my step I stop at the market for steak, potatoes, and green beans. I feel like making a big dinner after the great day I had. The bakery on the corner is bustling but I manage to grab a cheesecake and a bottle of wine with little hassle.

"Asald, are you here?"

The T.V. is quietly playing in the background but I don't see him anywhere. I drop the grocery bags on the kitchen table and notice he isn't here either. Making my way to the bedroom, I kick off my shoes and just start to pull my shirt over my head when I see him sitting on the fire escape. If it weren't for the slight rise and fall of his chest, I would think he had reverted to a statue again.

I knock quietly on the window frame and wave. His face lights up with emotion; I never knew what love looked like but I know that's what I see when he looks at me. How unfair, he has had a year to fall for me and I only just met him. For many seconds neither of us says anything, instead we stare into each other's eyes. I've never felt chemistry like this before, he is the sun and I may get burned getting too close to him, but that's okay, I'm ready for the adventure.

"Have you been out here long?"

"I was feeling a little closed in, I missed the air and the sun." His eyes close as he turns his face toward the setting sun, "I know this is one of your favorite times of day, want to join me?"

Awkwardly, I climb out the window and stand against the wall as he takes up most of the platform. His hand reaches for me and not sure what he's going to do, I lay my hand in his. He pulls me onto his lap and wraps his arms around my waist.

"You don't know how many nights I fought the urge to do this. Having you in my arms, unable to touch you was worse than any torture I had received in Hell."

"I still can't believe the things I confided to you. I wouldn't have said those things to my best girlfriend, let alone a guy."

"If it will make you feel better, I am giving you a free pass to ask me anything you want any time. I will always tell you the truth, no matter how embarrassing. Deal?"

I nod before turning back toward the sunset. In all the times we laid like this, I never felt such heat radiating from him. His breath lightly blowing on my neck makes me forget all about what we're supposed to be doing.

"It's gone now, ready to go?"

My eyes fly open, I hadn't even realized I had relaxed against him. I stand up quickly and climb through the window.

"I'm going to start dinner, you are welcome to help."

"Sure, I'll be right in."

The last potato is peeled when I hear him come in behind me. He clears his throat and out of the corner of my eye I see him standing awkwardly in the doorway.

"These are for you." He hands me a haphazard bunch of flowers and smiles sheepishly.

"These are lovely and they look like the same flowers Mrs. Martin is growing downstairs in her window box. How funny is that?"

"Yeah, that is funny."

"Did you by chance take these from her planter?"

"Technically, yes, but I did leave a note that I would pay her back when I have money so that's not stealing, right?"

The hopeful look on his face ends any argument I was going to say.

"They are beautiful, I'll put them in water and you start cubing the potatoes."

Once the potatoes are boiling, I put the steaks in the skillet and get the green beans going.

Without asking, Asald sets the table. I like that he came already trained.

Together we finish the rest of the cooking and sit down to a gorgeous meal.

"I feel like you know everything about me. How about you tell me about your childhood, what was it like living on a farm in the seventeenth century?"

"It was a horrible existence made better with a loving family. Everyone pitched in and helped each other. Dirty jobs always go faster when you have a sibling to commiserate with."

Over the next hour, I laugh till tears are pouring down my face. The pranks he used to play on his brother, the holidays his family took painstaking effort in making special. It's comforting to know his whole life hadn't been horrible.

With the last bite of steak consumed, he sets aside his napkin and lets out a small groan.

"That was most definitely the best meal I've had in a very long time."

My belly tightens when he stands and holds out his hand for me to take.

"Let me show you how much I appreciate everything you have done for me."

"But I have dessert."

"Your dessert is exactly what I want to get my mouth on."

"Oh."

His lips kiss my cheek, then lower to my neck. His breath against my skin sends shivers down my spine.

"Take me to your bed, let me pleasure you."

Being the suave girl that I am, I simply nod and walk shyly down the hall. I walk in and stand awkwardly next to the bed. I'm no virgin, but this is the first time I'm sleeping with a guy I barely know. Do I undress him or me or do we do each other? I really did not think this through very well.

His eyes never leave mine as he unbuttons his shirt and lets it fall to the floor. I reach behind me for my zipper when he shakes his head no.

His shoes and socks go next, then his pants and underwear. With two long strides he is wrapping me in his arms and kissing down my neck again. His hands glide around and slowly unzip my dress, pushing it over my hips to the floor. He moves lower and smothers his face between my breasts as his hands cup my ass and pull me against him. My hands in his hair, I hold him against me and a moan escapes when he unclips my bra and takes a nipple roughly into his mouth. He pulls on one, then switches to the other. I'm no lightweight so imagine my surprise and excitement when he lifts my legs up so I'm forced to wrap them around his hips. His mouth finds mine as he lays me down, his chest hair brushing lightly against my nipples, making them harden.

My clit throbbing for more attention, I can't help but grind against him. I love foreplay as much as the next girl but I need him inside me.

I can't take much more, I am about to beg for it, but I'm saved as he moves lower again and trails kisses down my chest to my abdomen, then to my hips and thighs. He smiles wickedly before sliding my underwear off, grabbing my legs and spreading me wide.

My eyes close instinctively as his tongue slowly licks all the way up to my clit. My hips move to their own rhythm, I need more. He latches on and sucks hard as my back comes off the mattress and I yell out.

He makes loves to my pussy while I writhe on the bed. One leg is released as his fingers slide inside my wet folds, torturing me with slow thrusts. Desperate for more, I yank his hair and he gets the hint, picking up the pace. Within minutes an intense orgasm is ripped from me and he holds on and sucks gently till every last wave of emotion is gone.

Out of breath and mildly embarrassed, I take a few deep breaths as he kisses his way back up my body and lays next to me. I peek at him out of the corner of my eye and see a huge grin on his face.

"You look mighty proud of yourself."

"I love hearing you finish."

"Was I really loud? I think I blacked out a couple of times."

"Let's just say Mrs. Martin won't even have to ask how your night went."

I grab the pillow and cover my face, I hear his bark of laughter and can't help laughing, too.

"Don't cover your face, I want to see you when I fill you."

I didn't think it would be possible to want sex so fast. Those words are all it takes to make my pussy start throbbing again.

Reaching into the drawer of my nightstand, I grab a condom. I have no idea what they used for protection in his time, it might be better to do this for him. On my knees, I straddle his thighs and stare into his eyes as I wrap my hand around his cock and stroke slowly.

There is nothing sexier than watching a guy's eyes cloud over, that moment when their brain shuts off and intense pleasure takes over.

Reaching down, I scrape his balls gently with my nails and chuckle when he bucks and moans.

"Please, I need to be inside you."

Rolling the condom on, I move up and dangle my breasts over his face. He takes one nipple in his mouth and the other is being tugged by his hand as I slide the tip of his head inside my body and move up and down slowly. His other hand moves from my breast to my hip and squeezes. I know he wants desperately to push me down so he's fully embedded inside, but I shake my head no and continue the torture.

"Jesus, Penelope, you are a temptress, aren't you?"

Leaning down, I kiss him deeply as I push down and take him all the way in. I gasp against his mouth. I've forgotten how good it feels to have a man inside me.

His hands dig into my hips as I speed up and within seconds he has taken over and I lose all train of thought as I am slamming down hard and fast.

His thumb finds my clit and with a few circles, I scream out and hang on while he growls out his own orgasm. Out of breath, I collapse against him and melt into a puddle of satisfaction.

"You have no idea how much I needed that," I mumble between heavy breaths.

"I am glad I could be of service. My compliments to the chef, dessert was amazing."

"That's nothing, wait till you taste my cheesecake."

"Don't mind if I do." Without a hint of exhaustion, he rolls us over and slides back in easily.

"Sweet Heaven, it has been so long since I've been inside anyone, yet it feels like the first time with you." His words whispered against my neck send chills down my body, "You've woken something inside me."

People say the darndest things in the throws of passion, he can't mean his words when he barely knows me, but it sure is an aphrodisiac to hear them.

His pace slower and more sensual, I languish in his attention till we both ride the crest of an orgasm together.

I stretch and roll over to watch him walk to the bathroom to clean up, his ass is perfection. I hear his stomach rumble across the room.

"About that other dessert I have, the one in the kitchen, would you like it now?"

"I could go for another helping."

He slaps my ass as I pass by. Standing at the counter cutting the cheesecake, I can't help sighing when he wraps his arms around my waist, kissing my shoulders.

We sit down and eat in contented silence and after a second helping, he clears the table and holds his hand out to me. Thinking we're heading back to the bedroom, I'm surprised when he turns me around and bends me over the table. I hear a condom wrapper open and he slides in easily. I hold onto the edge and relish in the pounding he is giving me.

With one final hard thrust, he shouts as he releases again and collapses against my back.

"My god, Penelope, what have you done to me?"

"You, what about me? I don't know how I'm going to walk tomorrow."

His bark of laughter makes me giggle until he swoops me up into his arms. I can't help the yelp of surprise. Like a prince from a fairy tale, he carries me to bed and tucks me in.

Fourteen

The week flies by and when I'm not busting ass at work, I'm home with Asald. We get along so well, I forget I've only known him for a couple of weeks. When he makes love to me, I want to cry and I feel every orgasm deep in my soul. As he comes, he whispers his love for me. I haven't reciprocated yet; there is no doubt I love him, I'm just not ready to give in so quickly.

His eagerness to catch up with the world and experience everything makes every day exciting. Today is no different, I rush home for our next date.

"Asald, I'm home, are you ready to go?"

"What exciting adventure are we going on tonight?"

He pops out of the kitchen with two glasses of wine in hand.

"Well, there's a fall festival going on so I thought we could go on some carnival rides and you can win me a stuffed animal."

"If that is your desire, I will win you one hundred dolls."

"I actually believe you would but my apartment just isn't that big, so how about just one really big one?"

"As you wish."

We finish our drinks and head for the train. His face lights up like an eager child when the carnival comes into view.

"I guess you are excited?"

"I've never seen a festival such as this, and what is that smell?"

"That, my friend, is fried dough, there is no better carnival treat. Down that aisle are more fried foods than you could ever imagine."

"I definitely think we should start there."

He grabs my hand and takes off down the aisle. Once we've collected a frozen lemonade, funnel cake, chocolate covered bacon and a turkey leg, we sit at a picnic table.

"There are so many choices, can we try more later?"

"Let's see if you are still hungry after all of this."

I tear off a huge piece of funnel cake and watch quietly as he devours everything else. His lusty moans cause heat to pool in my belly, those are the same sounds he makes when he is sucking on me.

"That was amazing, now it's time to win your prize. Come pick out the doll you want."

After a few stalls, I see the perfect one hanging beside stuffed dragons and wizards.

"That one is perfect, it looks just like you did."

I pay for the game and he smiles slyly when he's handed the balls.

"To win a small prize, you have to shoot four of the targets, a medium prize is six, a large is eight."

"How many to get that gargoyle?"

"You'd have to get all ten targets in one minute, and it's never been done."

With a decisive nod, he cracks his neck and grabs a ball off the pile. The carni starts the game and ducks pop up and start moving all over. For a full twenty seconds Asald does nothing, just stares intently. I've only been able to find seven of the ducks with targets, the rest are moving too fast. Finally, when I think he's just going to give up, he wings the first ball in and knocks the duck back.

In quick succession, eight more ducks go down. With fifteen seconds left, he has one left to find. I see his eyes scanning quickly, then a dimple pops on his cheek and I see another ball fly by. Bells ring, lights flash and Asald grabs me into a huge bear hug.

"I can't believe you got them all, that was awesome."

"Dude, how did you do that?"

He puts me down and turn his cheesy grin back to the carni.

"I have excellent hand-eye coordination and she's my good luck charm."

He reluctantly hands us the stuffed toy and turns his back on us, what a spoil sport. We walk away, proudly holding our prize.

"Seriously, that really was incredible. I could barely see some of those and you hit them like they were standing still. Thank you."

"Anything for you."

On my toes, I stretch and kiss his beautiful mouth, his tongue slides in seeking mine. Goosebumps run down my arms and makes me shiver.

"Are you cold? I'll hold the doll while you put on your sweater."

I reach down to my waist and remember I had set my sweater on the counter at the game.

"Oh shoot, I left it back at the game."

"No problem, stay here and I'll be right back."

I lean against the railing and watch the riders getting on and off the ferris wheel.

"Penny, is that you?"

David, date number four, walks up and gives me a hug. Odd behavior for a guy who promised he would call then completely forgot about me.

"Hi, how are you?"

"I'm good," I see him looking around anxiously, "I'm really sorry for what happened. I really liked you, I wish we could have gone out again."

I don't even know how to respond. He had my number, he kissed me good night, what was the problem?

Over his shoulder, I spot Asald bearing down on us and he doesn't look very happy. Before I can introduce him, he plants his arm across my shoulders and pulls me against him. The look of horror on David's face is terrifying.

"Are you okay? You don't look so well."

He completely ignores me as he stares at Asald.

"Look, man, I didn't know you were still with her. We're cool, I'm outta here."

They've met? I have a sneaking suspicion why none of my dates ever worked out. Jerking out of his grasp, I spin on him with fire in my eyes.

"What the hell was that? And remember, you have to tell me the truth."

"It's not a big deal, I just made it very clear that you aren't available."

"Oh my god, how many of the guys did you scare away? Did you scare off Marcus or did Hank?"

He had the good sense to look sheepish.

"All of them, except the last one. He was being just as sneaky as me and I couldn't catch him. I scared off Marcus and followed him to make sure he had left, I didn't know Hank was waiting to swoop in on you."

"You ass! I have spent all this time thinking there was something wrong with me. Instead, I have a neanderthal walking around, beating his chest and telling everyone I belong to him."

The image of him doing this enters my mind and a small part of me is actually turned on by it.

The larger feminist side is pissed and she always wins out.

"This is the twenty-first century, buddy, you don't own me." I snatch my gargoyle out of his hands and storm off. "Let's go home, and I'm warning you now, you are back on the couch."

Fifteen

"Psst, Penelope, are you awake?"

The gentle shake of my shoulder pulls me from a really good dream where Asald is on a spinning wheel at the carnival and I get to throw balls at him. I guess I'm still a little mad.

"I made breakfast for you. Well, I poured you a bowl of cereal, some orange juice and coffee, but I did it all with love."

I roll over and quirk my eyebrow at him, I'm not falling for that cutesy act.

"If I get up, will you stop talking?"

Without a word, he nods and heads back to the kitchen. What he did was wrong, I get it though. In his time men were more possessive and he was making his intentions clear. I'm going to forgive him after I teach him a little lesson about modern love.

After a quick trip to the bathroom, I find Asald sitting at the table with a place setting for me and another for the stuffed gargoyle. If it is the last thing I do, I will *not* crack a smile.

I slide into the chair and pour milk over my cereal without saying a word.

"So, what adventure are we going on today?"

"I'm not sure, I was just going to hang around the apartment."

"I want to do something for you, how about a picnic at Johnson Park? You can meet me there at twelve and I'll have everything ready."

He is a fast learner, "Sure, I can meet you there, how you are you going to pay for the picnic?"

"Good point. You know, if you don't want me stealing from criminals, I'm going to have to find some kind of work to do."

I look around and see my purse on the kitchen counter. Grabbing my wallet, I hand him my debit card.

"Remember when I showed you how to use this and I gave you the PIN?" I wait for him to nod, "Take it and buy whatever you need. I will see you at twelve."

"This is going to be great!" He jumps up, kisses me on the cheek and heads toward the living room. With a bite of cereal in my mouth, I see him pop his head back in, "Can you keep an eye on Frank and make sure he eats all his food? Thanks, love you, bye."

Like a tornado, he swept through and was gone just as quick.

"What are we going to do with him, Frank?"

His glass eyes stare back at me, kind of comforting actually. "I guess I better make myself presentable if he is going to all this trouble for me. Be good, Frank."

I shake my head at myself for talking to the stuffed creature and head to the bathroom for a long, hot bath. If Asald plays his cards right, I'll consider letting him back in my bed.

Sixteen

The blanket is spread perfectly under the tree and everything is ready. The wine is chilled and the meat and cheese is artfully displayed on the platter, along with plenty of fruit and a cheesecake for good measure.

It's almost one p.m. and she still hasn't arrived. I know she's mad, would she really stand me up? Frustration wins out and I pack everything up. I consider going to my pedestal to get away for a while but I'm too pissed. She had no right to do this to me.

Storming into the apartment, I toss the food on the table and growl at Frank's smiling blank stare.

"Penelope, where are you?"

Rustling in the bedroom gives her away. I stomp down the hall and stop in the doorway.

She's lying on her bed staring at me with fear in her eyes.

"What is it, what's wrong?"

Three steps into the room I see a movement out of the corner of my eye. The force of the blow sends me against the wall.

"You! What did you do to Penelope?"

"Every year on the anniversary of the day I imprisoned you on that roof, I peak in to remind myself how much I enjoyed doing that to you. Imagine my surprise when I stop by to find your pedestal empty. At first I just thought your statue had been moved. After some digging around, I came up empty handed. On a hunch I looked in on Arabelle's descendants and I find you shacked up with one of them.

"I admit I'm at a loss as to how you broke the curse, but I'm not going to worry about it. I should have obliterated you centuries ago. Now I can make up for that lack in judgement." The prince of Hell waves his hand and sends me flying across the room, and ropes snake around me till I can't move.

"Penelope dear, come here."

She fights every move her body makes, desperately trying to go against his will. She stops in front of me, tears rolling down her face. The prince moves the hair from her shoulder and kisses her neck.

"Why do you want to be with a farm boy when you can be with a prince?"

Her face slackens. Of course he's going to let her talk, it's no fun when he doesn't play with his victims first.

"You are a monster, Asald is ten times the man you are." The spark of anger in her eyes should be comforting but it scares me instead. He has the power to do whatever he wants with her, she has no idea how serious this is.

"I'm the monster? Do you know the things he did in Hell? He is just as sick and twisted as I am." Shock reverberates through my body when I see her spit in his face, she is tempting him and I'm afraid he won't mind torturing a woman like I do. "I like your spirit, maybe I will keep you around for a while. What do you think of that, Asald? After a few years, do you think she'll stop thinking of you while I'm buried deep inside her?"

A roar rips from my throat but the ropes are too tight, I can't do anything to help her.

"I will never let you touch me!"

Lanthos' laughter sends chills down my back.

"You really think you can stop me?" He waves his hand and a table appears next to us, all of the weapons I used for torture laying there, taunting me. His hand glides down her arm to her hand. He forces her arm up and grabs a knife.

"Breaking you will be my greatest accomplishment." Together their arms come up and the blade slices down my chest from my throat to my belly button. The cut isn't deep, he just wants to make me bleed. Tears run down Penny's face as she struggles, I can see the fear and anguish in her eyes. I will not yell out and cause her more pain.

Cut after cut, they mark my entire body, the pain is excruciating. "Now you will finish what I started. Cut his throat."

"No, wait, if I agree to go with you, will you let him go? I'll be with you if you promise to let him live out his life here in peace."

He throws his head back, laughing maniacally. Shaking my head, I beg with my eyes for her to stop.

"That is actually a better torture than killing him. I will agree to your proposal if you agree to consummate the deal in front of him." His eyes flick toward the bed, I can't watch this but I'm powerless to move or speak.

"Deal." She leans in and whispers softly, "I will always love you."

Lanthos grabs the blade and punctures my heart. I should feel pain but instead there is just cold. I can see Penny screaming but I can't hear it. He throws the bloody dagger on the table and strips naked as he walks to the bed.

"You promised you would let him live!"

"And I will, my dear. As soon as we fuck, I will heal him. Trust me, he won't die, I won't let him. Consider this an insurance policy to guarantee your compliance. I wouldn't take too long though, he is slowly bleeding out. Now, do we have a deal?"

Barely able to keep my eyes open, I see her lean against me and feel her warm lips on mine. "Just hold on, baby, this will be over quickly."

I watch as she takes her shirt and skirt off and sets them on the table of weapons. Nausea hits me as I watch her climb on the bed and straddle his hips. Her hands are shaking as she reaches back to unsnap her bra and a flicker of light catches my eye. She pulls out the bloody dagger that was tucked into her underwear. Glancing at the table, I can see the spot where it should be. I try to scream to stop her, she can't kill him and doing this will seal both our fates. The dagger plunges deep into his heart, he never saw it coming.

"Here's the thing about curses, fucker, true love trumps all."

The look of shock on his face as he convulses gives me hope that maybe she did hurt him. She climbs off and runs to me. Still holding the bloody dagger, she cuts the ropes and throws herself into my arms. We watch as the prince's body disintegrates into dust and disappears.

"Did it work, do you think he's really gone?"

Unable to stand any longer, I collapse to the ground. "Just hold on, I'm going to call 911. You are going to be fine. You've waited this long to live free of him, don't give up now."

"I should have known you would be at the center of this." The new voice in the room causes Penny to scream.

"All I can do is take small gasping breaths as the demon who made that fateful deal with me all those hundreds of years ago walks toward us with a gleam in his eye. "I am Lanthos' second in command. When you destroyed him, I felt it. I needed to see for myself, I needed to know what happened to finally free me from him."

"So it's true, I really killed him?" Penny's hopeful face stained with my blood and her tears turned pleading eyes on him.

"Well, killed isn't really the right word for it, he was technically already dead. The funny thing about true love is how pure and powerful it is. When he stabbed Asald, he made that dagger powerful, all of Asald's love for you attached to that blade. By stabbing Lanthos with that same blade, the magic entered his long dead heart and destroyed him from the inside out. I have to admit, I'm glad it worked, I've wanted to get out from under his rule for over a thousand years."

With one last gasp, I feel the moment my heart stops beating.

"No...no...no, you aren't leaving me now." She spins back to the demon, "If you are so happy to be free then please save him. If it weren't for him, you would still be working for that beast."

"You are right, my dear. Besides, when Asald showed up I was relieved of my torture duties so I'm grateful for that."

He waves his hand and each cut on my body slowly seals closed. With a huge gasp, I sit straight up, fully healed. "Now if you will excuse me, I apparently just got a big promotion. I need to go visit my new palace and start making some changes. Oh and consider our deal done. I am feeling generous, though, so I've given you a new ID and enough money to keep you both happy for the rest of your days."

We don't even notice him disappear as we only have eyes for each other.

"I'm so sorry I risked your life, I couldn't let Lanthos win. I actually thought if I did manage to kill him that you would automatically be healed. I am such an idiot."

Pulling her away from me, I grab her shoulders, "If that hadn't worked you would be dead, why would you risk yourself?"

Her hands wrap around my neck, pulling me down, "Because I thought it was about time the damsel saves the hero." Her lips find mine and all of the desperation, fear, and love are poured into that kiss.

"I need to be inside you, I need to erase any thought of him touching you."

"Sounds good to me, but maybe we do it on the couch. I think we should wash the sheets before getting back in that bed."

The sound of her laughter soothes my weary soul.

"God, I love you."

"Just think, it only took four hundred years for you to find me."

"And I would do it all again if it meant I get to grow old with you."

She unhooks her bra and tosses it to me. Stopping in the doorway, she turns back to me. "I was thinking maybe this time you could keep your wings out." She winks and walks out.

I hope you enjoyed Penny and Asald's story. To continue following their journey checkout www.blackhollowtown.com

The next book in the series is titled

<u>Reviving Love</u>

One

"It's been two years Sarah, they locked Hank up and threw away the key. Asald and I love you and we want to see you happy. Even Alex is starting to question your lackluster love life."

Sarah scowled at her friend Penny, how dare she insinuate her little boy was thinking about her dating life.

"All we're saying is you could use a weekend of adult time. My parents are going to keep Christian for us and they've offered to keep Alex too. Come with us to Black Hollow, Asald promises his friends are awesome and we're going to have a lot of fun."

Sarah's nails tapping in rhythm on the table seemed way more interesting than making eye contact with her best friend. She knew she was right, she had lived like a nun for so long now she didn't know how to break out of the prison she had built around herself.

"You trust Asald and me, believe me when I say Alex will be safe and you will have fun. Besides you know you're as curious as I am to meet his friends. We've talked to them so many times on the phone, they'll be offended if you snub them and don't come."

"Well, that's not fair, playing the guilt card on me." Sarah sighed as Penny wiggled her eyebrows, smiling like a loon. "Fine, if I agree to go with you this weekend can we agree that I don't have to be forced into another dating situation for at least six months?"

"Six months! That's crazy." Penny exclaimed as Sarah quirked her eyebrow and leveled a hard stare that froze Penny in her place, before finally relenting. "Fine, six months free from our intervention into your sex life."

Satisfied with her agreement she gave in. "So, tell me about this grand weekend you have planned? What do I need to pack? Where do I call for a hotel room? And where the hell is Black Hollow, Massachusetts, I've never heard of it."

"I haven't been there before either but I can't wait to go. It's a small coastal town just North of Salem. From what he's told me they are even more eccentric than Salem and celebrate all kinds of paranormals not just witches. They throw this huge Halloween party every year that is by invitation only." Sarah grabbed a towel and started drying the dishes Penny was washing. "We are staying at an Inn and I already booked you a room next to ours."

"Someone was confident I was going to cave."

"More like determined to hound you till you let me have my way. We're also picking up costumes in town so don't worry about packing anything special. All you have to do is meet me at my parents Thursday after work and we'll drive up."

Childish laughter filled the room as Asald came into the kitchen with their son Christian on his shoulders and Alex wrapped around his leg being dragged.

"Good news babe, she's going with us this weekend." Asald's look of surprise meant he hadn't expected his wife to be successful either.

Asald pulled his leg forward so he could see Alex's face. "I guess that means you are playing big brother to Christian this weekend. Grandma and Grandpa have lots of fun things planned and really want to you stay with them. What do you think?"

Alex popped up off the ground and melted his mother's heart with a huge smile. Two years ago they'd been living in a shelter, abused and alone. Now they had Asald and Penny and their entire family had adopted them. She would be forever grateful to Penny's parents for treating him like any of their other grandchildren. Tears burned her eyes; she swallowed hard around the lump in her throat.

"Can I stay with them, mom?"

"Of course, you can. Now grab your backpack and let's get home."

"Bye Birdman!"

Sarah shook her head at Alex's nickname for Asald and hugged everyone goodbye.

***

As soon as the front door closed Asald gave Penny a look of concern. "Are you really sure you want to do this? Are you ready for her to know all about me and my world?"

"For two years Alex has sworn you can fly and saved him on that roof. She has never believed him before so I don't think she will suddenly figure things out after one party. However, I hate keeping this one huge part of our life a secret from her so I'm hoping to break it to her this weekend."

"I trust you so if you are ready for her to know the real me than so am I. Now, let's get Christian in bed and go work on making him a little sister or brother."

Two

Sarah stood staring at her closet, it was hard to pack for the unexpected. At least she was used to Fall in New England so it wasn't tough to throw in enough layers to make an outfit for any situation. Hoping she had grabbed enough choices she left to meet up with Penny at her parents' house to drop the kids off. This was the first time she would be sleeping away from Alex and the idea paralyzed her. She was relieved that he was excited to be going, this meant his father hadn't completely destroyed him.

"I'm really doing this aren't I?" Penny rolled her eyes at Sarah's mumbled and repeated question.

"Would you like some liquid courage to help calm you down? We can fill a thermos before we go?"

"No it's fine, I'll be fine, let's just get on the road so I can't back out." Sarah saw the compassion on her friend's face, Penny had seen

Sarah at her worst, her most broken and understood how big of a step this was for her.

They pulled into Penny's driveway as Asald was putting the last of their bags in the trunk. After a quick kiss for Penny, he grabbed her bags and moved them to his car. "Okay ladies, let's do this."

He practically ran around the car to get going, he was meeting these friends for the first time as well. From what Penny told her, Asald had been doing some kind of genealogy research and found a group of people who were similar to him. She assumed that meant maybe their ancestors were from the same area or something? She wasn't really sure when she pushed them for details they mumbled a bit then moved on. Was there a skeleton in his family tree he didn't want to talk about? Either way, she was glad he was making new friends, like her, he was an orphan and had no family so she hoped these people would change all of that for him.

She watched out the window as the miles went by, her mind wandered until she jerked awake realizing she had fallen asleep.

"Welcome back sleepy head, you were out for a while. We just got off the interstate, it won't be too much longer now."

After a few turns, she noticed the beautiful oranges, reds, and yellows of the leaves had faded and everything was either brown or barren. It was actually breathtakingly beautiful seeing the naked branches reaching across the road towards each other almost like lovers reuniting. The buildings they passed weren't shiny or new and the town all but took her breath away. She knew they catered to tourists by playing up the paranormal but this was amazing.

The apothecary had signs in the window exclaiming a sale on love potions. The blood bank had fangs with dripping blood in their logo. Competing bars on the corner had signs listing who wasn't allowed in their establishments. Stoney's on the left didn't allow witches, fairies, or any other creature that were not part animal. Thirst had one very clear rule: no animal shifters of any kind could enter.

At the stop sign, she heard Penny gasp as a group of children crossed the street all holding brooms and each had an animal with them. One of the kids black cat was jumping towards another girl who had a Raven perched on her shoulder. The boy at the end was barely swinging his cauldron, probably because the largest toad in history was peeking outside of it.

"When I fell asleep did we cross into another dimension? This is incredible. I've visited Salem, they have nothing on this town." She couldn't help the double take when she saw a perfectly normal looking girl serving coffee outside of 'Hells Brew'. She didn't seem fazed at all standing in front of two large men with black wings lightly fluttering while they sipped their coffee.

"The guys said the town goes all out for the month of October. Everyone gets involved and plays up their characters, I guess they weren't kidding." Asald gave Penny a nervous glance. She thought it was cute, he seemed hesitant to meet his friends.

They turned off the main road and followed a street around to a surprisingly quaint looking Inn that didn't seem to fit in with the rest of the town's aesthetic.

"The Daydreamer Inn, this looks pleasant." Penny's reassuring smiles gave away how nervous she was about their accommodations being a rundown looking motel.

Penny and Sarah each grabbed a bag while Asald grabbed five. She was always surprised by his strength; she had seen him do some crazy stuff when he was working out or fixing things.

Their attention was turned away from Asald's bulging muscles when the door swung open, soft music reached their ears. No one came out to greet them, Asald looked at them, shrugged and went up the steps.

The Inn was even more beautiful inside. She didn't know if it was the music or the paint color but as soon as they entered a feeling of calm and safety washed over her. Behind the counter was an ancient looking man, his fine silk pajamas seemed like odd business attire till he introduced himself as Mr. Sandman. How was this town not a year-round theme park? His slow speech and deep rumble were relaxing as they followed him to their rooms.

"We have very few rules here but they are important ones. Do not go into the cellar, the dragon who lives down there is a noisy fellow but he minds his business so I let him stay. The windows are never to be opened, even if you think you hear music, the banshees like to play with visitors and trust me you don't want to get involved with them. Lastly, the sprites and brownies are excellent housekeepers but they can be naughty. If you leave them some chocolates, they will usually leave you alone."

If anyone else had been speaking that would have taken less than two minutes. With his slow drawl, it had been almost ten. He turned to leave them at their doors when she noticed he wasn't wearing shoes, instead, he had a pair of thick socks on. "Oh, and if you should have trouble falling asleep call the desk, I have just the thing to help you." With a slight bow to them, he turned and went back downstairs.

"Oh my god guys, thank you so much for forcing me to come along. This place is amazing."

"I admit it is so much more than I expected as well. Get settled in and we'll leave for dinner at seven."

Sarah gave Asald a mock salute and unlocked her room with the real, iron key Mr. Sandman had given her. Like the rest of the Inn, her room was beautiful and comfortable looking. She was surprised to see a definite lack of technology. Hopefully, they wouldn't be in the room much, she wasn't sure she knew how to occupy herself without a T.V.

As soon as she closed the door she couldn't help but jog over and do a back flop onto the giant marshmallow mountain of a bed. The satin sheets were more luxurious than anything she had ever owned. She was grateful the Innkeeper took such great care to make sure they had the best sleep possible.

After a quick phone call to check in with Alex she closed her eyes and enjoyed the silence. She hadn't been alone in years; the lack of noise was surprisingly deafening.

A knock on the door broke her focus, "It's just me." Penny's face appeared upside down over hers. "You look comfortable, explains why you didn't realize what time it was."

"I can't leave now, the bed has accepted me as part of it and I don't want to move."

"Ladies, let's go. We're going to be late."

"I know you love your new bed but Asald is getting antsy so up you go."

With a heavy sigh, she raised her hands. Penny walked around the bed and yanked her up. "Okay, okay, let's go."

Three

A short drive back through town took them to a restaurant set back from the main road. The stonework of the building gave it a medieval feel. Large lanterns hanging every few feet put off a tremendous amount of heat from the flames within. They were greeted by a hostess wearing a corset dress made out of large scales. She would hate to see the alligator those must have come from.

Sitting around a large round table were three giant men, she had thought Asald was big but he was average sized compared to them. Smiles instantly transformed their faces as they saw them and jumped up to crush them each in hugs.

"Finally, we meet!" Two of the giants looked alike, she assumed they were the brothers Pascal and Toussaint. The third man was calmer, standing back watching everyone, it was safe to assume this was Aristide, the one who owned a bookstore.

"We're so glad you all finally came up here. This is the best week of the entire year so you are in for a real treat." The brothers held out chairs for Penny and Sarah to sit in.

"There is no seat for Sebastian, is he not coming?" Asald looked between the three friends curiously.

After a couple of odd looks between them, Aristide made an excuse that he had to work. You would think being the Chief of Police would let you take time off when you wanted to.

A waitress dressed like the hostess passed out menus and took their drink orders. After ordering, Sarah excused herself to the restroom. At the back of the restaurant, her attention was caught by voices coming from behind a partition. Always more curious than she should be she peeked behind the temporary barrier.

She had never seen such beauty before, the man sitting at a table deep in conversation stole her breath away. Tiny silver lines crisscrossed every inch of skin she could see. They shined with his movement, it was a beautiful sight.

She must have gasped, his head turned sharply and their eyes met. Seeing his face filled with anger didn't penetrate her thoughts as his beauty sent a shiver down her spine. Her fingers itched to trace the tiny scars running across his forehead and cheeks.

"Ma'am, may I help you with something?" Her transfixion was broken by the deeply tan man with black piercing eyes standing next to her in the hallway. "That is a private party, can I help you find your way back to your table?"

"Oh, I'm sorry, I was actually looking for the restroom."

"You are in luck; one more left turn and you will be at your destination."

Embarrassed at being caught she nodded and scurried away without a backward glance at the man who was sure to take over her every thought. Deep in her stomach, she felt a burning need to know who he was and what happened to him.

***

"Dinner was amazing, the charring on my steak was perfect." Asald leaned back and rubbed his still completely flat stomach.

"I agree, the smoky flavor of my chicken was excellent." Pascal set his napkin aside and waved over the waitress. "Can you let Pietr know we are ready for dessert."

Sarah's plate was removed as she spied the dark stranger from the hallway approaching their table.

"Pietr, so good to see you again. Did you enjoy that book I sent over last week?" Aristide talked more animatedly than he had all evening, it was obvious books brought him to life.

"Thank you for finding that for me, it is definitely a rare treasure." Intense black eyes found hers and smiled. "I see you found your way back to your party?"

Sarah couldn't help the blush she felt burning her cheeks.

"I heard you all are ready for dessert, allow me." Pietr leaned in and removed the center of the table which turned out to be a cover for a large burner. With a cheeky smile and a wink to Penny, he put his hands to his mouth and blew fire into the burner igniting it immediately.

Penny grabbed Sarah's arm as they both let out a gasp. "How did you do that?" Sarah couldn't help but laugh with excitement and intrigue.

"A little dragon fire to make your dessert more luscious." With another wink and a small bow, she watched as he went to the back and disappeared behind the temporary wall.

What she wouldn't give to follow him and see the sexy stranger again.

"That was incredible, how did he do it?" All four men at the table shrugged, fat lot of good they were.

Waitresses brought a pot of chocolate and skewers for everyone. A few minutes later trays of fruit, marshmallows, and small square cakes were set around the table.

She watched as Toussaint speared a marshmallow and held it over the flame browning it before dipping it in the melted chocolate. Asald grabbed a giant strawberry and dunked it completely in the chocolate before shoving it all the way in his mouth.

If she wanted to experience the moans echoing around the table she had to dive in before it was all gone. She selected an orange segment and covered it in chocolate, intense flavor burst in her mouth as soon as it touched her tongue. The sweet chocolate mixed with the tart flavor of the orange was unexpectedly delicious.

Less than ten minutes later the trays were empty and the chocolate bowl was wiped clean. With one last groan of ecstasy she sat back, for a fleeting second, she imagined unbuttoning her pants for a little relief.

"That was amazing, thank you for picking this place." Penny licked the last drops of chocolate off her fingers.

"It's the best place in town, I always think it's weird to eat at the mermaid's place. Their specialty is fish and chips and that is just too cannibalistic for me." Toussaint laughed hysterically.

"You all do take this paranormal stuff seriously don't you?"

"It's a lifestyle." Pascal winked at Asald before erupting in laughter.

"So, what are your plans tomorrow?" Aristide ever the somber one asked with a more serious tone.

"Besides exploring more of the city, we have to get our costumes for the ball Saturday night."

"That's right, it's imperative that you dress to impress. You must go to Seraphine's Disguise. She has the best shop in town and has a knack for picking the perfect costume to match the monster that is inside you." Toussaint wiggled his eyebrows at them before laughing again. They really were a merry band of brothers.

"If you guys want to meet up tomorrow give us a call." Aristide hugged each of them before leading them out of the restaurant.

She couldn't help looking back one last time at the partition hiding the private party.

She was surprised to see Pietr talking with someone behind the barrier, he turned and stared directly at her while he continued to talk. With another blush at being caught, she took off after the rest of the group. How will she ever sleep tonight with visions of that beautiful stranger haunting her thoughts?

ABOUT THE AUTHOR

Cassidy lives in the Tampa, Florida area with her high school sweetheart, their three children, one crazy senior dog, a guinea pig, a skinny pig and the newest love of her life her puppy Flynn. She loves reading and going to the movies but not nearly as much as she enjoys watching her kids either playing ball or performing with one of their instruments. She also loves travelling and hopes to one day watch a baseball game in every MLB stadium in the country.

To learn more about Cassidy please visit her online at

www.cassidykoconnor.com.

You can also find her on Facebook at

www.facebook.com/cassidykoconnorauthor

She always welcomes new friends and encourages readers to reach out to her.

Other Books by the Author

Sassy Ever After

In My Mate's Sight

In My Mate's Defense

Paranormal Dating Agency

My Oath To You

Stand Alones

Broken Dreams

Forever Yours, Casey

The Laird's Promise

To Steal a Prince's Heart

Wicked Wonderland Retreat

The Love's Protector Series

Awakening Her Desires

The Evolution of Sam

Finding His Swing